ABANDONED

BY TIM WALKER

A LIGHT IN THE DARK AGES

PART ONE

(second edition)

Contents

Foreword

Abandoned is the starting point of a three-generation story of a family who must use their wits and skills to survive in post-Roman Britannia in the fifth century. The Romans made an orderly withdrawal from their most northerly province in the years leading up to 410 AD, after which the island reverted to tribal rulers and was beset with invaders from all sides, precipitating a bloody and destructive slide into a time of fear and uncertainty. A time of opportunity for some, and anguish for others. This story forms part one in the *Light in the Dark Ages* series.

The early part of the Dark Ages is a period of myths and legends, most notably of King Arthur. It is the realm of archaeologists and historians who search for clues to what actually happened in a turbulent period from which few written records have survived. It was the age of a desperate struggle for survival, wedged between the end of Britain as an orderly Roman province and the establishment of Anglo-Saxon kingdoms.

The idea for this story came about during a visit by the author to the site of Silchester - once the Roman town of Calleva Atrebatum in Hampshire. The site, maintained by English Heritage, is a square patch of grass surrounded by the remnants of an earth bank and broken outcrops of a stone wall. There are no surviving structures on it save for a Christian church added after its mysterious abandonment some years after the Romans departed. In 1866 excavators discovered a bronze eagle buried beneath the forum, thought by some to be an ornament whilst others speculate it may have been the standard of a Roman legion. Who buried it and under what circumstances remains a mystery. This bronze eagle – the inspiration for Rosemary Sutcliffe's *The Eagle of the Ninth* – a tangible relic from Calleva, also makes an appearance in this story.

Although much of the action in *Abandoned* centres on the town of Calleva, the starting point is Britannia's capital and largest town, Londinium - with an estimated population of around 40,000. From here the Governor ruled the province from imperial buildings clustered around a forum at its centre and it would most likely have been the embarkation point for the final withdrawal from the province.

Abandoned

MAP AND PLACE NAMES

Roman Britannia—Main Roads and Towns

Calleva Atrebatum – Silchester in Hampshire
Noviomagus – Chichester (south coast port)
Venta Belgarum – Winchester
Aquae Sulis – Bath
Corinium – Cirencester
Isca Augusta – Caerleon (South Wales)
Londinium – London
River Tamesis – River Thames
Stanes - Staines

Camulodunum – Colchester
Verulamium – St. Albans
Glouvia – Gloucester
Isca Dumnoniorum – Exeter
Lindum – Lincoln
Eboracum – York
The Wall – Hadrian's Wall
The Gaulish Sea – The English Channel
The Germanic Sea – The North Sea

4

PART ONE: GUITHELIN

Chapter One

HOLDING UP THE hem of his brown woollen habit, the elderly bishop tutted as his sandals sank into soft, cold mud, engulfing his toes. His young novice delicately held the back of his habit as they sloshed through a puddle between the stone bridge approach and the wooden landing stage. Bishop Guithelin was determined to speak to Rome's most senior representative before he moved from his sedan chair to the pier and up the planks that would take him onto the imperial galley moored there.

He could now see the bald pate of Lucius Septimius, the departing governor of the southeast quarter of Britannia – Maxima Caesariensis – whose capital was here, in Londinium. Accompanying him were the Fiscal Procurator and regional administrators from Flavia to the northeast, Secunda to the northwest and Prima to the west. This was how the Romans had ruled their wild and windy northern-most province of Britannia – by dividing it into four manageable quarters. He stepped up to the wooden planks of the pier and hurried past slaves carrying bundles of clothing, boxes of crockery, gourds of wine and rolls of tapestries, to a line of Roman guards in their polished armour and plumed helmets, checking all who approached the ships.

Guithelin took a moment to gather his thoughts before attempting to pass through the line of soldiers. He noted the liveried slaves in woollen smocks wearing leather sandals – their masters certainly knew how to maximize on their investment. Many Britons did not have such fine and practical clothing, the poorest making do with cast-off pieces of canvas roughly sewn as shoes. He studied the faces of the slaves who passed – lined with the marks of toil – Britons mostly; men, women and children, with evenly cut brown hair. Did they know they would be sailing away soon, most likely to never see their homeland again? He straightened his habit and positioned his silver cross in the centre of his chest before he boldly approached a tall, officious centurion.

"State your business!" the centurion barked at the tiny tonsured bishop.

"I am Bishop Guithelin of the southern diocese. I must speak to the governor..."

"The governor is busy with his inventory. Go about your business," the burly officer said, looking down a pronounced nose and clutching the hilt of his gladius sword with practised menace.

Guithelin cleared his throat and replied in an authoritative tone, "He has forgotten a valuable item that I have in my possession and he would not thank you for keeping it from him." He fumbled in his pocket and produced a leather pouch.

"Give that to me and I'll pass it to him," the dark-eyed officer demanded, holding out his hand.

"I shall not, and you must let me pass!" the spirited bishop replied, raising his voice so that others noticed. The centurion studied him closely and, deciding he posed little threat, stood to one side.

"Be quick now – neither his Excellency nor I wish to spend any more time than is necessary on this filthy island."

The short, stout bishop crossed himself in self-admonishment for the lie, returning his leather pouch to his pocket as he strode towards the huddle surrounding Governor Lucius.

"Your Excellency!" Guithelin cried as he approached the elderly Roman official standing beside the gangplank. Lucius recognized him, but his sour look was not welcoming. He turned away to encourage his family members standing close by to board the vessel before rounding on the holy man.

"What is it, bishop? I have already prayed in your church with my wife and family and received your blessing. It is now time for our departure..."

"Your Excellency, I wish only to say my last farewell and ask your advice," Guithelin replied, fidgeting with the silver cross that hung from his neck.

Lucius motioned his clerk to come forward and handed a parchment to him. "Speak then, dear bishop. I had grown fond of your sermons in our Roman tongue, often amused at your inclusion of Briton words where your knowledge of our language failed you."

Guithelin was used to the Roman ways and merely smiled benevolently. "You are kind, Excellency, and correct to point out my shortcomings. But it is on the matter of the future governance of this city, indeed this island, that I wish to seek your counsel."

"My dear bishop, you must know that Rome has many troubles and we are being recalled by the Emperor Honorius to bolster the imperial army closer to our home. We leave behind no interests and have no opinion on how this province should be ruled after we have departed. In the words of our Emperor, you must look to your own defences."

He smiled like a man relieved by the removal of a heavy burden, who was now looking forward to well-earned respite. "You may move into my villa if you wish, and now..." He turned to leave, but Guithelin grabbed the edge of his purple robe.

"Your Excellency," he blurted. "Your words, so eloquently stated, confirm my fear that Rome harbours no plans to return to this province. In which case, I would seek your view on whom you see as a fitting ruler for this city – indeed this province?"

Lucius glared at him and pulled his cloak free. "I care not, bishop. Perhaps yourself? Either that or convene a council of tribal leaders. But then you are stuck with that barely-literate preening fool, Mandubracius of the Trinovantes and, even worse, Adomarus of the Icenii. Good luck to you!" He turned his back on the tiny man and boarded his ship, leaving the perturbed Briton and his novice standing in the midst of busy slaves and sailors, all eager to load the ship and make the evening tide.

Guithelin trod warily on the wooden pathway that seemed to float above the sticky grey mud beside the choppy waters of the River Tamesis. As his track joined the main causeway, he stopped to catch his breath and look up at the stone walls of the fortified town, noticing a gallery of faces on the parapet staring down on the final evacuation. Briton townsfolk mainly – there were few guards to be seen.

"Many will be glad to see the Romans go," he commented to his silent novice. Despite the chill of autumn, he mopped his sweaty brow with a delicate embroidered cloth and turned to see the gangplank withdrawn as the shouts of overseers prompted oars to slide out of holes in the galley. The large vessel glided slowly out into the main current and headed for the gap at the centre of the bridge where twin drawbridges had been raised to allow it to pass. Smaller boats accompanied it as the last Roman fleet moved downriver towards the ever-widening estuary and the open sea.

GUITHELIN SAT IN the governor's chair in his office in the Basilica, facing a dozen Briton clerks and minor officials who could read and write and knew something of Roman administration. He had recorded their names and professions on a parchment and now looked up to address them.

"My dear brothers, I thank you for answering my call to this meeting. Our Roman masters have gone, but our town of Londinium, indeed the territory surrounding it they called Maxima Caesariensis, still remains. They have shown no care for who rules in their wake, and so I, on the suggestion of the departing Lucius - and after lengthy prayer - have been guided to try and bring order to our town and outlying areas." He surveyed the row of concerned faces, all men whose ages ranged from barely twenty to sixty years.

"To this end, I would convene a council from those of you in this room, for the purpose of organising civic services and tax collection..."

"But on whose behalf shall we collect taxes?" a white-haired elder asked.

They all turned at the noise of the doors being roughly forced open. A group of determined warriors strode across the marble floor, over a tiled mosaic of Poseidon riding the waves, scattering the toga-clad clerks.

"On whose authority do you call this meeting, Bishop?" a tall noble demanded, his wild curls barely contained by a leather headband.

"Welcome, my lords Mandubracius of the Trinovantes and Adomarus of the Icenii. It is God the Almighty who has guided my hand in calling a meeting of clerks and administrators who are wise in the ways of organising what needs to be done to run this town..." Guithelin had risen to his feet, bowed slightly in deference and crossed himself at his mention of God.

The stocky Adomarus had pushed forward to stand beside his taller neighbour, glaring at the tiny bishop with black-eyed menace. "You cannot assume any authority in this land, bishop," he growled.

Mandubracius smiled down at him and turned to Guithelin. "Your concern for order is commendable, bishop. However, my friend is right. We are now the rulers of this land, and the tribal boundaries, over which the Romans imposed their provinces, will be restored. In this area, known previously as 'Maxima', the chiefs of the Trinovantes, Icenii and Cantii will take on their inherited responsibility to rule their peoples and their land."

10

Silence fell on the room. Guithelin gathered his thoughts and replied, "My lords, it was ever to be the way. I merely show a concern for the effective running of this town that has grown as a trading port of some stature, and must be governed…"

"Must be!" Adomarus cut in. "The Romans have gone and we will now rule as we see fit, in the ways of our forefathers."

Once again, Mandubracius turned a pacifying look on his fiery fellow chief.

"But you are both right," he said. "The town must be managed and the people put at their ease. Also, taxes must be collected and the walls and gates manned by guards. This we know, dear Guithelin. To this end, I shall lead a council of chiefs who will make decisions on weighty matters, and you, bishop, shall run your committee of clerks and report to me." He fixed his steely gaze on Guithelin, fingering his sword hilt and grinning at the prospect of ruling and having taxes collected on his behalf.

Guithelin felt the heat rise on his neck. Looking at Mandubracius to avoid the expectant gaze of his underlings, he gripped his wrist, gritted his teeth and nodded his reluctant acceptance.

"It was ever to be this way, my lords," he repeated, bowing to their backs as they departed.

Chapter Two

THE WALLED TOWN of Londinium was divided into two halves by the Wal Brook, which ran south towards the River Tamesis, its steep muddy banks crossed at two bridging points. Roman citizens and merchants had lived mainly in the western quarter in villas with gardens. In the north-west corner was an enclosed barracks that could accommodate a legion of five thousand men, positioned beside a large stone gatehouse. From this gate, Watling Street ran northwards, cutting a straight line through the heart of the island. Many of the wealthier Romano-Briton families had also gone, choosing to relocate to the relative safety of Armorica in north-western Gaul, their villas now occupied by a handful of traders and those seeking grace and favour from chief Mandubracius. The crowded eastern quarter housed Britons, Picts, Gauls, Saxons and a multitude of noisy, smelly livestock in muddy pens.

Guithelin stood on the porch of his wattle-and-daub church, which was close by the main bridge over the Wal Brook, eyeing with envy the sturdy stone building that was once a place of worship for the mystical god, Mithras, and was now a tavern and brothel. It was frequented by Mandubracius's unruly guards and had become a focal point for debauchery in the town.

He signalled his elderly curate, Waylin, to join him. "You have witnessed much change in this town, dear brother – what can you tell me of that building?"

"Your Eminence, it is not like any other temple that the Romans built to honour their gods. Mithraeism was a secret cult favoured by soldiers, and they would meet to hold rituals involving sacrifices to their bull-killing god, Mithras."

"But have you been inside?" Guithelin asked.

"Indeed, my curiosity got the better of me and I crept in the day after it was abandoned by their priests. It is a dark place, sunken in the earth to resemble an underground cave. There is a long, narrow room with a raised altar at the far end cupped in a circular enclave. Two rows of columns support the high arched roof and behind the columns are dark corridors that I believe were used for... privacy, Your Eminence."

Guithelin looked at the building and imagined the interior. "Then it would make a suitable place of worship once again, with the faithful arrayed on benches facing a high altar. Our simple building has served a purpose, but now we must look for a new home that is sturdy and big enough for a growing congregation. I will speak with our chief about ending this debauchery and returning this fine building to a place of worship."

Enthusiasm for the worship of the Roman gods had waned and their priests had all joined the evacuation. There were some followers of Druidism attempting to revive the old beliefs, but Guithelin knew this was a time to grow his Christian following and offer spiritual guidance to the people in a time of uncertainty. "Now I am Mandubracius's chancellor I believe my knowledge of fiscal matters affords me some bargaining powers," he muttered.

He wrapped his cloak about him and made his way past two-storey townhouses, livestock pens and a flour mill where a pair of docile donkeys trod a circular path, towards the largest building in the town – the Basilica - where his chief held court. It was one a number of imperial buildings that lined a square of compacted earth known as the Forum. He hurried past the bustle and cries of market stall traders selling dried fish, caged birds, pigs, vegetables, flat breads and cakes to housewives and slaves who bartered for a good price with small coins bearing the heads of long gone Roman emperors. He paused to catch his breath before ascending a flight of a dozen stone steps and passing into a shaded portico lined with Corinthian columns and on through the double oak doors, nodding to a disinterested guard crouched beside a burning brazier.

"Ah, my chancellor, come closer," Mandubracius said, waving away a group of farmers who were perhaps involved in a land dispute.

Guithelin approached the raised dais and bowed to his chief. "Greetings, my lord. I trust all is well?"

An eerie quiet had descended on the townsfolk in the weeks following the departure of the last Roman fleet. Mandubracius had settled comfortably into the governor's villa and office and had moved his extended family and loyal guards into the legion barracks. He had recruited more guards from neighbouring tribes and the odd assortment of foreign drifters living in the town to man the gates and walls and was now dealing with ancient land feuds that had resurfaced after the Romans had quashed them.

"As well as can be expected," he said, turning to give the bishop his full attention. "I trust your tax collectors have been busy?"

"Indeed, my lord. Although revenue is much reduced from Roman times due to the lack of trade and fewer wealthy merchants and landowners. However, we are blessed that life continues and we are at peace."

Mandubracius adjusted a bronze armband and leaned forward to fix his hazel eyes on the small figure before him. "I need coin to pay the guards and feed my court, dear bishop. To this end, I am giving you my brother, Gwethin, to oversee the collection of taxes. I am disappointed with the paltry amount you have so far handed over and feel you would benefit from his help in this matter."

His muscular brother stepped forward, silver clasps swinging from his forked beard, ridged tattoo swirls on his cheeks. Guithelin bowed to him and turned to his chief, squeezing his hidden wrists in the sleeves of his habit.

"My lord, your brother will see for himself the problems we face. On another matter, may I be permitted to move my church into the Temple of Mithras?"

Mandubracius threw his head back and laughed. "And now you ask me for a favour? Well, I will consider this after the next tax collection, although I understand it is now a tavern popular with my men. If there has been an increase in coin, then perhaps I will consider it. Now go and explain your methods to my brother."

Guithelin spend a difficult hour with his tax collectors trying to explain the methods, frequency and amounts collected to the illiterate Gwethin. His brow was set in a look of deep suspicion, and he erupted angrily when symbols that meant nothing to him were referred to on parchments.

15

"My brother is only interested in more coin!" he shouted.

"We collect from farms on the rise of the new moon, and from the levy on traders at the gates," Guithelin explained. "You can accompany my collectors next week when they ride out to the farms and see for yourself what can be collected."

"And I will place my own men at the town's gates to collect from the traders," Gwethin growled, before marching away with his guards.

Guithelin turned to his perturbed assistants and said, "This is how it will be from now onwards. Their lust for coin is insatiable and they will take it by force if necessary. I fear we will not have a share to buy oil for the street lamps or attend to other civic matters. We must be on our guard and not get drawn into disputes. I will pray that God's wisdom enlightens them."

THE STORMS OF winter kept merchants in their ports and farmers in their homes as the market stalls of Londinium grew sparse in their wares. Angry words and fights broke out as prices were hiked for increasingly scarce victuals. Tax collection had not yielded as much as Mandubracius had hoped. It had started at a paltry amount and steadily declined to barely a trickle, and Guithelin, thwarted in his desire to convert the Temple of Mithras to a Christian church, now feared for his safety as the town descended into rough rule from soldiers under squabbling tribal leaders.

Over dinner in his modest tiled house with his curate, Waylin, his oldest administrator and two young priests, he shared the thoughts that troubled his mind. "Our situation is grave and will only worsen. By spring, many of our townspeople will leave this place to eke out an existence on farms."

"Aye, and to escape Mandubracius's thugs who are making life intolerable," Waylin added. They sat in silence as the bishop's housemaid ladled out turnip soup into their bowls.

"We have fallen far from Roman standards," the old man said between slurps of soup.

"They will not be back and we must make our own future," Guithelin replied.

The youngest priest, Father Damian, chewed on a piece of turnip, spitting out the mulch. "And spring tides may bring unwelcome visitors from Gaul and Saxony," he said, picking his teeth.

"Aye, pirates will add to our troubles for sure," the old man croaked, soaking in his bowl a piece of the hard bread he could no longer chew.

"There must be something we can do to halt this slow slide into tribal conflict and the threat of invasion?" Father Damian asked, looking hopefully at his bishop.

Guithelin considered his reply before giving it. "I have an idea. I fear we shall be overrun by determined invaders who will see how weak and defenceless we are without Roman legionaries to oppose them. They will lay waste to our ports and soon sweep inland to trouble our people. Our chiefs are more concerned with their boundary disputes and in amassing wealth. They will not protect us. We need to find a new ruler who is of noble birth - a Christian who knows his letters and has a care for the lives of the people."

The group stared at him, digesting his worrying prognosis. The old man stoked his white beard and cackled. "Dear Guithelin, is there such a person on this island? The wealthy have gone and the only educated people remaining are ourselves and a few others. Even now they are burying their coins for fear of raiders. This is another reason why your tax collections are poor."

The stocky bishop solemnly replied, "There is no one I know of on this island who can unite the tribes. Each chief will have his own interests at heart. We have witnessed that in the behaviour of Mandubracius who has quarrelled with and expelled the Icenii and Cantii from this town. Their chiefs are now licking their wounds in their tribal strongholds, envious of the plunder that has been denied them and plotting their revenge. No, I must take ship to our enlightened neighbours in Armorica and plead with King Aldrien to come and claim this land as his kingdom. This I have seen in my dreams and believe it to be the will of God. Aldrien is known as a fair and saintly ruler of a civilized country. I charge you all to aid me in this endeavour and speak of this matter to no one. It is our God-given duty to gather souls for Christ, but we also have a responsibility to do what we can to protect our flock from the wolves who gather about them."

A CHORUS OF larks greeted Bishop Guithelin as Waylin helped him load his bags onto a cart in the rear yard of the church where he had spent a sleepless night. The warm spring morning air was welcome after a cold and fraught winter. He glanced around the corner of the church but saw only early morning traders pushing carts towards the Forum.

"Make haste, father," he called in a loud whisper to his travelling companion, the young priest Damian, who had agreed to accompany him on his journey. "I fear Gwethin may come at any moment and would not take kindly to my leaving."

"You are his money pouch, master, and his anger will scorch those around him when he learns of your journey," Damian replied, checking the pony's bit at the front of the cart.

"May God bless and protect you," Waylin said, holding open the gate for them.

Guithelin blessed him as they departed and turned to his companion. "We must hurry to the east gate and pray that our Christian guards will be there to let us pass." He had been planning his journey for several weeks but knew the hardest part would be leaving Londinium undetected. He was forced to take two guards who were regular parishioners into his confidence, and now must test their faith. He sat at the front of the cart, cloak wrapped tightly and leather brimmed hat pulled down, as Father Damian led the pony by its bridle through still sleeping narrow streets, the only sound the squeak of the miller's wheel as mournful donkeys strained in the yoke. They followed a circular path that skirting the Forum and took them to the east gate.

Father Damian had forsaken his monk's habit for the dress of a trader – cloak with hood up over a quilted doublet and woollen breeches, his shins tightly bound with leather cord above sturdy walking boots. He led the pony gently towards the stone gatehouse in the shadow of twenty-foot high walls, looking about him in the quiet gloom of the early morning.

"Hail fellow," he said to a guard lolling in the shadows, partly obscured by smoke rising from a brazier. The guard stepped forward into a patch of light, holding a spear and shrugging his shoulders under a grey wolf skin blanket.

"Who goes there?" he demanded, clearing his throat. Guithelin looked up from under his brim to see if he recognised the fellow. He did not.

"We are townsfolk looking to hunt and gather firewood from the forest. May we pass, good sir?" Damian asked, smiling at the unkempt man who stood scratching himself. The guard did not reply and looked doubtfully at the pair whose clothing and speech clearly did not match that of the servants or slaves who regularly journeyed to the woods. He approached the cart.

"I will first see what you carry beneath your canvas."

"I know these people." A voice from the gatehouse caused all three to turn. Guithelin sighed his relief as his parishioner stepped into the light, adjusting his belt buckle. He walked to the other guard and offered him a boiled egg. "They often pass here and make camp in the woods."

The first guard grunted and lost interest in the contents of the cart, staring instead at the egg in his palm. "Very well, let them pass."

"God be praised," Guithelin muttered, nodding to his parishioner as they passed through the arched gateway and followed a track that would take them to a fishing village on the north bank of the Tamesis, downstream from Londinium.

"We shall soon set sail for Gaul, master, and God shall guide us across the sea," Damian said, throwing off his hood and smiling at the frail elderly man behind him.

"We shall need God's guidance and protection to avoid the storms that whip up and pirates who plague our shores," Guithelin replied, glancing over his shoulder at the silent stone walls at his back.

Chapter Three

"IT IS CALLED 'The Castle of Light' in your Briton language," the ship's captain shouted above the noise of crashing waves, pointing to a rocky island on which stood an imposing stone fortress, its conical tower caps pointing regally to the blue sky.

"It is a magnificent sight," Guithelin replied, wrapping his cloak tightly as offshore winds whipped up white caps at the rocking prow. The helmsman yelled at the six crew to lower the single mast and run out their oars as he expertly guided the trading vessel beside a wooden pier bustling with activity. Guithelin pressed some silver denarii into the captain's hand and shuffled warily down the gangplank, holding onto Father Damian's sleeve. Their bags were dumped beside them on the pier by sailors eager to load the barrels and packing cases that awaited them for their return journey to Londinium.

The captain shouted down at them, "We must hurry to make the tide. You will have to wait in the village until the tide goes out, and the causeway to the castle will appear like magic from the sea - God speed, fathers, and pray for our safe passage!"

"There is no magic in this, only man's inspiration guided by God's wisdom - goodbye dear friend and safe journey!" Guithelin and Damian hiked their packs onto their shoulders and dodged along the pier, past eager labourers earning their keep. Father Darren led the way, holding up his cross to those they passed, and they were soon guided to a Christian church on the outskirts of the village.

A portly priest in grey habit greeted them and ushered them into his rooms at the rear of the stone building. Guithelin was impressed with the sturdy and permanent nature of the building, hinting at a long and stable history free from pagan raiders. The priest introduced himself as Father Gaius and they were soon conversing in Latin. Their well-fed host's housekeeper served them a rich broth of meats and vegetables with flat bread and boasted of regular attendance at mass of over two hundred, often with latecomers standing outside the crowded church. Collections were generous from the fearful sea traders and fishermen who sought God's protection from pirates and the elements, enough for him to employ farm workers and keep fowl, cows and sheep.

"God has indeed blessed you, dear father," was all Guithelin could say between slurps of the delicious broth. He exchanged looks with his companion – they could only dream of such a congregation and abundance of God's grace and favour.

"In one hour the tide will be out and you may cross the causeway to the castle. You will find King Aldrien a very devout and welcoming king. He is greatly loved by his people," Gaius said, a broad smile rarely leaving his chubby face.

"Are you his chaplain?" Guithelin asked.

"Oh no, his own two priests sing the Mass in the chapel at the top of the castle, and Bishop Troyes is a regular visitor. But I will accompany you, your eminence, and introduce you."

Refreshed, the group set out, Father Gaius riding on a donkey. Guithelin and Damian refused his offer to also ride, as the castle was in plain sight barely half a mile away. Gaius insisted his attendants accompany them and carry their bags.

"Oh, for a diocese as safe and wealthy as this," Guithelin whispered to Darren as they admired the well-tended fields and well-stocked fields on their journey. The causeway was now visible to them. It was paved with flat stones and stood raised above sucking sand and rock pools, pointing a straight line towards the arched gatehouse that stood beyond a drawbridge over a deep ravine.

"The Franks have only tried once to invade the castle, but soon gave up after losing many men to the quicksand and drowning by the rapidly returning tide," Gaius chortled from the back of his donkey.

"The village was not so lucky," one of his attendants added, earning a glare from the fat priest.

"It is a wondrous sight," Damian said, looking up at the turrets that jutted out from the walls. A trail of villagers accompanied them across the causeway, carrying baskets of fish, vegetables and other wares. Father Gaius smoothed their way past the guards and they entered the lower level where townsfolk bustled around market stalls that lined the main street that wound upwards, past tightly-knit dwellings and the occasional livestock pen towards the palace above. They were challenged by guards at a second gatehouse that led onto the summit where villas with well-kept gardens and orchards clustered around a palace of white stone.

Gaius explained, "The Romans built this palace for their governor and the villas for their officers and administrators. Now it is in the possession of King Aldrien and Queen Veralia who have united the Armorican and Benoician people through marriage to form a powerful alliance."

The weary travellers were met by a court official, who invited them to rest on marble benches beneath a portico supported by Greek columns that looked out on a flower and herb garden. Guithelin smiled at the sound of the gentle splash of a fountain, buzzing bees and the flutter of birds over colourful blooms in the calming scene before him. They were offered sweet mead and cakes by toga-clad servants and asked to wait until the king would see them.

AFTER A BRIEF respite they were escorted by guards to the twin doors of the main hall. They entered into a space of light, with high oak beams supporting a lime-washed ceiling and colourful tapestries hanging between long windows. It reminded Guithelin of the cathedral in southern Gaul where he had been ordained. They were led across the open space by a waddling Father Gaius to a raised dais where the king and queen sat, surrounded by courtiers.

"Ah, Your Eminence the Bishop of Britannia, you are welcome," King Aldrien said, smiling as he waved away his attendants.

"Your Majesty, my humble thanks for receiving us," Guithelin replied, bowing low. "If I may correct you, I am merely the Bishop if the Diocese of Londinium, one of four bishops on our island where God's holy word has spread across the land. May I introduce my companion, Father Damian."

Aldrien preened his pointed brown beard and regarded the curious and dishevelled pair, who clearly had not changed their clothing in several days. Indeed, murmurs ran around the room at the introduction of Father Damian as he was dressed in the manner of a trader.

"News of the final departure of Roman administrators from Britannia has reached our ears, confirming claims, that all was not well, by legionary deserters who had not been paid for some time. Pray tell us the situation that now pertains on your island?" The royal couple, resplendent in golden robes studded with fine jewels, held hands and sat back, awaiting a response.

"Your majesties are well informed and understand the fragile situation our island finds itself in following the departure of Rome and their soldiers. For some years the Romans had been troubled by raiders from Gaul, Saxony and from above the Wall of Hadrian and also from the western isle of Hibernia. They had built fortresses to try and protect their blighted Province but grew weary of the task and have eagerly answered the Emperor's call to leave us and defend the borders of Gaul and elsewhere."

"But surely, they have left your people strong and schooled in sound governance?" the queen asked, sounding hopeful.

"We were mere vassals of Rome – the Pellegrini – whose value was only in our labour to our masters. That they took many of our young men with them when they departed shows how little regard they had for our survival and leaves no doubt that Rome has prioritised its own protection above all else. We have indeed been abandoned. In truth, there are many pagan peoples living outside the bounds of Rome's empire who are hostile to Rome and who now seek to ravage our land."

"This is a sad lament," Aldrien said, leaning forward and waving at his attendants to bring chairs and refreshments for his guests. "Please sit and continue, Bishop Guithelin, as I feel there is more to this tale. Tell me about the Briton nobility and their plans for their defence."

Guithelin settled into his chair and sipped water from a cup, conscious of the close attentions of the finely dressed courtiers on both sides. "My lord, the three local tribal chiefs have looted the temples of Londinium and surrounding places and put on me to collect taxes for them with little interest in civic matters. They have argued and fallen out amongst themselves, and I fear they have little interest in good governance over the people, nor in providing protection for them from emboldened and determined raiders."

The gathering courtiers were enthralled by his carefully crafted account that employed both common Celtic phrases and Roman words, whispering to each other to ensure they understood the meaning. He took another sip of water and waited until the murmurs died down.

"I am here, lord, to entreat you to come to the aid of the poor remnants of the people of Britannia and come with force to claim the kingdom that is yours by right. For you are of noble birth and are a wise, fair and God-fearing king who can restore order and dignity to our troubled land."

Silence fell about the room as the king and queen exchanged startled looks. They leaned close together and talked in whispers. Guithelin and Damian sat back and picked figs from a platter. After a minute Aldrien cleared his throat and spoke.

"There was a time before when I would not have refused to accept the island of Britannia if it were offered to me; for I do not think there was anywhere a more fruitful country when it was at peace. But now, since it is falling into calamities, it is of less value and odious to me and, no doubt, to other princes."

Guithelin squeezed his wrists in front of him inside his wide sleeves and looked crestfallen as muttering once again echoed around the hall. Aldrien raised a hand to silence his followers and continued, "Nevertheless, out of respect to the ancient rights my ancestors held claim to over your island, I shall charge my brother, Constantine, with the task of leading an army to your shores, to free your country of barbarians and to take the crown for himself."

Father Damian could not contain his joy at this pronouncement and leapt to his feet, clapping his hands furiously, prompting the courtiers to erupt in laughter. The mood was lightened, and the smiling king raised his hands to still the noise.

"This will take some time to arrange as Constantine is now patrolling the borders of our lands with a force, charged with keeping the Franks at bay. Once he is returned, we shall sit and discuss the matter with him, and the size of the force he is able to lead. To that end, we shall start to recruit from the families of exiled Britons and Roman legion deserters who live amongst us. Until that time, you shall remain with us as our guests."

Aldrien and Veralia promptly stood to take their leave, ending the audience. All bowed before them and a lone trumpeter conveyed their retirement to the royal apartments.

Father Gaius escorted his guests through a side door and along a path to a chapel. Guithelin was deep in thought and paid little attention to Gaius's prattle as he pointed out tapestries woven with fine gold thread and candlesticks of carved silver on an ornate marble altar. He broke off from his cataloguing of the finery around them and said, "You will be saying Mass here whilst you await the return of Prince Constantine."

Guithelin looked up at him with sharp eyes. "And what can you tell us of the character of Prince Constantine?"

Gaius stared at him for a moment and then chuckled. "King Aldrien is the older brother and is scholarly and thoughtful. Constantine, the younger, is more impulsive and has chosen the way of the sword over the scriptures. Like most brothers, they disagree much and frequently quarrel."

"I see," Guithelin said, massaging his wrist. "Then perhaps King Aldrien would be glad to see his brother gone from his court."

"A threat removed, perhaps?" Father Damian added.

Gaius fidgeted and looked around conspiratorially. "You say threat. I say I suspect both king and queen would be glad to see the energetic prince embark on an adventure to a foreign land. Also, due to his nature, I feel Prince Constantine would be a suitable leader of the, well, savage Britons." He glanced at the altar and added, "Perhaps our Lord God has prepared him to meet this challenge." He smiled to himself – pleased to have found his way to a devout conclusion.

"Indeed," Guithelin ruminated. "It will be a challenge and he will need to show his mettle before our NOBLE chiefs." He tried to shame Gaius for his earlier slight, but the fat priest just chuckled. "Let us offer up our prayers, Father Gaius, that Prince Constantine will succeed in unifying our troubled land."

"...And that Armorica remains safe from invaders in the absence of our warrior prince," Gaius added. The three tonsured priests knelt at the altar rail and fell into silent supplication, hopeful of a sign that they were guiding the hands of their lords into acting out the will of God.

PART TWO – MARCUS

Chapter One

POLYAMIS LOOKED UP from his position on his hands and knees at the magnificent polished bronze eagle with outstretched wings. He sat back on his haunches to get a better look and stretched his aching back. Scrubbing the wooden floors was one of his many tasks in the villa of centurion Flavius Vitus, garrison commander at Calleva Atrebatum in the heart of Britannia Prima. Polyamis marvelled at the intricate workmanship and was forever in awe of the proud eagle in constant readiness to fly away. He was a house slave who could only dream of escape and his flight back to his village on the shore of the blue Aegean Sea. He rubbed the crude eagle brand on his arm, his master's mark of ownership, as he stared at the secret symbol of freedom.

"Get back to work, wretch, and stop day dreaming!" The hand of Cassius, head of the household, slapped the back of Polyamis's head, catching him off balance and sending him forward onto all fours.

"Sorry master, just stretching my back," he muttered. A kick up his backside was the only response.

Polyamis was clever but tried to hide it. He was also a thief and had amassed a store of stolen items in the pit under the main living space in the villa, which was raised on wooden piles to encourage warm air to circulate. He longed to take the bronze eagle and add it to his collection. One of his jobs was to fetch fresh water from a well close to the west wall. Here he would meet other house slaves who would share gossip or simply moan about their poor treatment and harsh lives. On one such morning, he met with his friend, Camillus, a slave in the household of the town magistrate.

"Hey Poly-anus!" his burly, dark-skinned friend whispered hoarsely, checking around for any prying ears, "have you heard the news about the evacuation?"

"What are you talking about? It is only a muster of the second legion as they pass by our town marching to the east. There is no evacuation, surely?"

The big man grabbed his arm. "My friend, I have overheard my master give instructions to the head slave that he is to pack up all things of value, including the town's rolls, and place them into carts this very evening, and keep it quiet, under pain of death." He widened his eyes in a mix of excitement and dread.

"Surely this cannot be," Polyamis replied, unhooking his pail of water from the hoist and resting it on the circular stone wall of the well. "We have had no such instruction. You had best not repeat this to anyone else, or death may indeed be your reward. I will see what I can find out."

With that he walked away, leaving his friend in the queue to draw water with other jabbering slaves, knowing they would most likely meet again in the afternoon. As he strained to carry the heavy pail using both hands, he noticed some urgency, soldiers and messengers running rather than walking through the streets of Calleva – home to three thousand souls, of which five hundred were Roman legionaries comprising the third cohort of the second legion.

In the late afternoon, Polyamis returned to the well to again draw water. Sure enough, Camillus was there, conspicuous not only for his height and bulk, but as the only black-skinned man in town.

"What news, my friend?" Polyamis whispered as he stood behind him.

Camillus looked around before replying, "We will be leaving this town for good just before dawn, so as not to alarm the locals. I will accompany my master and his two ox carts. Something has happened in the Roman world, but I do not know what it is."

Polyamis stared up at his friend. This report confirmed his suspicion that a general evacuation was underway. "My own household is also in secret preparations. It is my intention to try and escape in the darkness before dawn. Are you with me?"

The big man stood straight and drew a deep breath, staring over Polyamis's head as if searching for his answer. "I had not thought of it," he said. "Do you have a plan?"

"Only to hide at the moment of departure. They will be committed to leaving and will not have the time to search for runaway slaves. I will hide under the house and only come out once they have left the town gates." He looked about to make sure no one was listening. "Then I would make good my escape to the forest and hide there until such a time as I know what has happened in this province of Britannia."

A slave girl, Prisca, joined the queue behind Polyamis. A crude shoulder-length haircut did not undermine her natural beauty. The sway of her hips drew many admiring looks and he would often flirt with her at the well. As Camillus drew his water, Polyamis turned to her and said, "Pretty Prisca, our Roman masters will be leaving this town tonight. I intend to hide and flee to the woods. Will you come with me?"

She stared back in wonder with wide doe-like brown eyes and gasped. He put his hand on her arm to calm her. "I...I don't know, Polyamis. It is a dangerous idea..."

"But you must know your household is preparing to leave?"

"Yes, another posting for my master, perhaps?"

"No! It is a general evacuation. Even the magistrate is going, and no doubt the town elders. This is our chance to escape and I would take you with me."

He stared intently into her eyes. She blushed and looked away. Camillus winked as he walked past. Polyamis began to lower his pail to the water far beneath the town. She stood close by him, not sure whether to stay or go. He completed his task in silence and whispered to her before their ways parted. "Hide under your house just as they are ready to leave and wait for me. I will look for you." With that he walked away, joining the busy main street, weaving past drovers and cattle to his master's villa.

A CRESCENT MOON rocked like a boat on troubled seas as dark clouds scudded across the night sky. Polyamis looked up from the colonnade around the courtyard and deemed the time was right. He had finished loading the last of the wagons and went back to his master's study with an old red cloak to take down the bronze spread eagle from its perch. The room was empty of ornaments, save for the watchful eagle mounted on a pole, and only discarded furniture remained. He worked the bronze cast free from its support, wrapped it up and then checked there was no one in the corridor. He sneaked out with the red bundle in his arms and headed not for the courtyard but for the kitchen, where a cupboard housed a trapdoor into an underground room.

Pausing only to listen, he dropped down four feet to the dry soil base and pulled his bundle in, replacing the square of wood above his head. A cord tied to a hessian bag of root vegetables was pulled over the trap door. Groping in the dark, he found his way to a mat put there the day before, and gathered to him his sack of food, gourd of water and bag of precious objects he had stolen over the past year. He listened intently, but only heard the scratching of scurrying rats on the edges of the damp, square space. Satisfied that they were not searching for him he started to scrape a hole using a knife blade and a broken terracotta tile and buried his treasure, including the eagle, hoping he would live through the adventures that he felt now awaited him to return and claim them.

"Where is that wretch?" Centurion Flavius Vitus hissed in a hoarse whisper.

Cassius, his head slave, looked about wildly before answering, "We cannot find him, master. He has disappeared."

Flavius indicated Cassius should kneel and stood on the slave's back as he mounted his horse. He was in full military uniform, including a lavish red-plumed helmet. "We cannot wait. It is time."

He led two ox wagons, carrying his family and possessions, out of the gates of the villa contained within the walled enclosure of the barracks. On the parade ground, his troops stood silently in ranks in the pre-dawn gloom. His four optios stood to attention as he bent and whispered his order that they should follow. Within a matter of minutes, the garrison's five hundred legionaries, their supplies, slaves and personal effects following in a wagon train, marched out of the north gate and joined the road heading east towards the Portway.

Chapter Two

WHILE POLYAMIS PLANNED his escape, some fifty miles away Marcus Aquilius and his men watched in silent horror as seaborne raiders butchered everyone in their path. The cries of men, women and children slashed with swords, stabbed with knives, chopped with axes and bludgeoned with hammers filled their hearts with dread and anguish. The brief resistance of a handful of native Briton auxiliary guards had been brutally snuffed out by flaxen-haired invaders, who now rampaged noisily through the town, looting, murdering and burning the once busy town of Noviomagus Reginorum.

Marcus scanned the scene before him and noticed no evidence of Roman legionaries having been involved in the fight. "This town was named for the Regnii tribe, but without the protection of a Roman cohort they have been unable to protect themselves," he muttered.

Marcus signalled his troop of thirty men to slowly move away from their position on the cliff top and return to their horses. There was nothing they could do to help. It was all over. The brutish invaders moved like hungry wolves over the bodies of the dead, picking what loot they could find.

"Where are the Roman legionaries?" a disconsolate soldier cried. "My cousin Pick is amongst them!"

Marcus had no answer.

His task was to report back to his commanding officer, Flavius Vitus, garrison commander at Calleva Atrebatum, that this was no small raiding party. There were six long ships in the harbour, each able to bear fifty-or-more warriors – a sizeable war party, and one that would most likely take the long, straight road to their own town, once their lust had been slaked.

"The Romans did too good a job, linking their towns with roads for ease of supply and rapid movement of soldiers," Marcus observed, as his disconsolate men reached the picket line and prepared to mount.

Drustan grunted and added, "But now this advantage will be used against us by raiders such as these who will follow the dusty roads to slaughter, mayhem and a fortune in gold and silver."

The sun was starting to dip as they set out on the journey from the coast to Calleva in thoughtful silence. A dozen or so fleeing locals followed behind them. Marcus took careful note of the terrain through which the road passed, his mind already alive to some kind of defensive strategy. They stopped at an inn, accurately named the Halfway House, as the evening drew in. Marcus decided to rest for the night and warn the occupants of the invaders. They set off before dawn as Marcus was anxious to report to his commander.

When they crested the final hill, apprehension gripped them as they noticed a dust cloud in the early morning light, leading them to push their tired horses into a trot. Reaching the lip of the plateau they could see the gatehouse, stone walls and wooden ramparts of Calleva, which nestled in the centre of a clearing cut from the forest, with roads running in four directions from well defended gatehouses. Plumes of dust away to the east indicated the movement of soldiers or a wagon train.

"Look, my lord, the garrison is leaving!" Drustan, his stocky deputy, pointed to his right at what looked like the entire cohort of the Second Legion disappearing into the tree line, followed by ox-drawn carts of supplies and camp followers. With visible despondency the troop of Roman auxiliary cavalry, a mix of Britons of the Atrebates tribe and half-blood Romans, spurred their horses towards the south gate. It had been a fortified Roman garrison spanning six relatively peaceful generations, a place of safety that dominated and administered a wide territory. Now their hearts were filled with trepidation and bad omens hung in the air, like the wheeling kites above them, waiting to pick at their soft white flesh.

Marcus Aquilius, their leader, was both Roman and Briton. His father had been a Centurion of the Fifth Legion whose bones now lay somewhere to the north, no doubt buried near the site of his last posting – a fort on the great wall of the Emperor Hadrian. He had his father's looks – black curly hair and dark brown eyes, easily tanned skin and a powerful build. His mother, Morcant of the house of Atrebates chief, Tincomarus, was a healer (and to some, a sorceress), widely respected for her knowledge of herbs and potions. He would seek out her wise counsel on these worrying developments that threatened to rock their orderly and peaceful existence.

They rode past agitated townsfolk to their stables in the army barracks, horrified to see the gates flung open and it empty of soldiers. Looters scurried about with arms full of furniture, trinkets and ornaments. Marcus detailed his men to seize the looters, recover what they could and secure the barracks whilst he went to find someone in authority. The garrison commander's office was ransacked and empty, and

Marcus back-handed a yelping boy, grabbing a stool and a cushion from him. He could read Latin and might need those maps and documents. Had rumours of a Roman withdrawal from Briton to fight in Gaul come to pass? Was he now the most senior military figure left in the town? He must act like it until told otherwise.

Marcus looked through the documents and found something very interesting. Breaking the seal, he read his own orders, scripted in the hand of Flavius Vitus, to fall-in with his troop of auxiliary cavalry, attached to the third cohort of the Second Augusta Legion, and make their way to an eastern port for evacuation to Gaul.

"Lucky for us we were out of this place for three days past," he muttered under his breath.

"What was that, sir?" Drustan said. Marcus had not seen him hovering by the open door.

"Keep the men together and ensure the gates and towers are manned," Marcus commanded. "We must keep the peace until I find out what has happened."

The town was in uproar, and Marcus followed the crowds to the forum, a natural meeting place in the town centre. On his way he passed the stone pillars of the temple of Mithras and the more modest wood and thatch Christian church. Both were assailed by wailing worshippers, prostrating themselves before their idols, seeking comfort and divine guidance. There was much confusion, and his own house was empty apart from two servants, whom he armed and told to defend it from any looters, on pain of death. Stern-faced, he went to look for his family.

Marcus passed between two stone carvings of emperors long gone, who gazed impassively over his head, and entered through an archway into an open central courtyard, pushing through the crowd. Would the gods of the Romans protect them from ravaging barbarians? He already knew the answer. Inside, a scene of anger and confusion reigned as the townsfolk divided to his left and right into two groups, each led by the rival sons of the local chieftain. To his left was Valorian, eldest of the two sons of Tincomarus, the Atrebates tribal chief who was now old and bed-ridden and counting down his final days. To his right was the younger son, Vortigern, a sly and cruel youth, resentful of his elder brother. Their constant squabbling had led to their ailing father granting them both lands to keep them quiet and away from each other.

Marcus knew that a time of chaos and uncertainty would be a time of opportunity for Vortigern and his unruly mob of followers. He made his way to Valorian, pushing through the throng of frightened toga-clad citizens, aware that his Roman officer's uniform still carried some authority. As he mounted the steps where the elders usually sat, he heard his mother's cry and turned to see her with his pregnant wife, Cordelia.

They were standing high up on the second tier, above the noise and confusion of the townsfolk now milling about the sandy courtyard, where the town elders would debate and plays would be performed. The upper viewing gallery above them was steadily filling with murmuring townsfolk and farmers. He waved to them and moved on. Valorian welcomed him warmly and gave him a goblet of watered down wine to slake his thirst. Marcus drank and it soothed his parched throat.

"Marcus, my friend, I am more pleased to see you than ever!" He signalled him to sit down in the seats formerly occupied by the garrison commander and civic elders. How often had they witnessed plays from ancient Greece and Rome acted here? Instead, the scene before him was one of mass confusion, of fearful people, their numbers swelling by the minute with the arrival of nearby villagers and assorted travellers.

Valorian spoke quietly to him. "I have grave news, my friend. The Romans have all been ordered to evacuate to Gaul. The Emperor Honorius has instructed his legions to defend Gaul from an army of barbarians approaching from the east, and they have taken a great number of our own men with them, leaving our town, and indeed our island, undefended from raiding savages from all sides – I hear reports that the Scotti attack the western shores, that there is trouble at Emperor Hadrian's great wall and soon the Saxons will surely invade us from south and east. I will need you and your men to organise our defences, but first, I must deal with my troublesome brother."

"My lord," Marcus replied, "I also have grave news. The Saxons have already come with a large force, some three-hundred-strong, and have burnt the port and town of Noviomagus, slaying the townsfolk and our gallant comrades and kin in the Auxiliary. They destroyed all in their path - looting, raping and burning - and must surely follow the road to our gates."

Valorian swayed backwards, his eyes wide in horror; "this is indeed grave news, my friend, but hush your voice lest you cause more fear amongst our people. They will be comforted by the sight of you standing by my side. Now I must bring my brother to heel or we will all be doomed to the same fate. Come, stand beside me."

The Forum had filled with several hundred people; anxiety hung in the air. Valorian stepped forward and raised his arms for silence. His guard of twelve Roman-clad soldiers, a close brotherhood of bastard cast-offs trained as soldiers from an early age, banged their swords against their shields to get the attention of the boisterous crowd.

"My dear friends," he shouted to quell the din, "I bring heavy news. As you can see, the Roman garrison has departed and is unlikely to return." Exclamations of shock echoed in the forum. He again raised his hands for silence. "We have enjoyed peace for many generations under the protection of Rome, but now we must look to our own administration and defences. As eldest son of my ailing father, the noble leader, Tincomarus, paramount Chieftain of the Atrebates, I claim the right to rule this town and the surrounding area." He glared across the arena at his sulking brother, Vortigern, who elected to stay silent.

"Those of our tribe who already occupy places in the Senate will continue, and new worthy citizens will be appointed in time, so there will be a continuity of administration and justice. There will be no looting of buildings, nor grabbing of property that belonged to the departed Romans." Murmurs and accusatory pointing broke out. "Housing will be allocated according to position, and all stolen items must be handed in by nightfall under my amnesty. Thereafter, any searches by my men that recover stolen goods will result in arrest and punishment of the offender." He glared defiantly at the mob, knowing that those who did not steal or came too late would turn on those who had.

"We must look to our own defences! To this purpose I appoint Marcus Aquilius as Garrison Commander." He raised Marcus's arm to a roar of approval from the crowd. Marcus stood tall and proud, but inside felt the uncertainty of youth, for he was yet to see his twentieth year. The young firebrand Vortigern stood as if ready to speak but his supporters pulled him back. This was not the time. Marcus gazed across the arena and noted those faces around Vortigern.

Valorian moved to make his closing remarks. "Dear friends, many of our young men marched away with the Romans to fight barbarian invaders in Gaul, leaving our numbers short. We have barely sixty trained guards and soldiers, roughly speaking half of whom are auxiliary cavalry, the rest gate guards and my father's escort. We urgently need every household to put forward at least one able bodied man or woman for military service. I appeal to all of you to heed this call. I have received word today that our sister town, Noviomagus, has been ravaged by a Saxon war party, and we must look to our defences in these troubled times." Cries of fear and anguish erupted as many had relatives and friends in that unhappy port.

He again tried to still the crowd and shouted to be heard, "Please! I implore you! Have faith in our ability to defend ourselves. Marcus will organise our defence. In the morning, all who will serve in our new army must report at the gates to the barracks. All will be accommodated and fed, as will farmers and their families who bring into our town stores their harvested crops and livestock. We must prepare for a siege! Go now and make your preparations! Hail Tincomarus! Hail Atrebates!" The response was muted and the crowd moved sullenly about their business.

Marcus found his family in the crowd and embraced them all. Everyone was full of consternation and fearful at the prospect of having to defend themselves without the skill and might of the Roman Legions. Valorian had instructed Marcus to move his family into the vacated villa of the former garrison commander, within the enclosed grounds of the large army barracks. He detailed his troop of horsemen to do the same and occupy a barrack block with their families. There were three empty barrack blocks and a mess – enough space to accommodate and feed a legion – where he would billet his new militia.

Marcus was pleased that Valorian had shown wisdom and decisiveness in his words and actions, as he knew that time was against them and the Saxon threat was real and imminent.

"Will the Saxons come, my lord?" Drustan had appeared at his side.

Marcus calmly replied, "They might stay on the south coast plundering, but before long will eye the long straight road to our door. They know the Romans have gone, and this fair land is defenceless and ripe for the picking. You must help me maintain calm."

Drustan banged his forearm across his chest in a robust salute. Marcus slapped his shoulder, smiled and turned to lead his family through the archway and out into the street, picking their way past urgent neighbours to their house.

Chapter Three

POLYAMIS STOOD ON the edge of the forest looking across an open stretch of cut, dewy meadow to the eastern walls of Calleva. To his left stood the abandoned amphitheatre outside the town walls. He was one of eight slaves, five men and three women, who had escaped the town as the soldiers had marched away. They had been living in the forest, catching small birds and squirrels, and foraging for edible plants, roots and bulbs. Between them they had the skills to identify foods, prepare meals and build shelters. Polyamis had asserted his leadership over the group and established their camp, taking the pretty pale-skinned house slave, Prisca, to his bed of leaves under a makeshift shelter of branches and moss.

"This way," he announced, leading them out of the shade of the trees into the open. They walked in the early morning spring sunshine to the back of the walled amphitheatre and worked their way around, ducking down behind a low wall in case any sentries spotted them from the walls. It had been two days since Marcus and his band of riders had returned. Since then a steady stream of the wealthier citizens had been leaving through the north gate and taking the road to the west. This had all been observed by the runaways from the dark forest edge.

"The merchants and their families leaving is a sure sign that the soldiers are not expected to return," Camillus had noted as they made their plans the night before. Some of the group was for staying in the forest or moving northwards, with the intention of joining a band of forest-dwelling outlaws and deserters.

"We should return to the town and offer our services to the lord Valorian, and ask to be made free men and women," Polyamis had argued. "It is safer in the town than out here."

The women had agreed, and his big friend, Camillus, had shrugged his shoulders. He was too far from Nubia to even contemplate a return home.

After some mutterings, a man called Januarius said, "We will follow you, for we would not be here if it wasn't for your escape plan."

"Which was supposed to be a secret," Polyamis said, looking accusingly at Camillus. The big man just smiled and shrugged.

Polyamis led the group in a crouched shuffle along the low-walled pathway joining the armphitheatre to a wooden door in the east wall. They passed busts of emperors and gods mounted on Corinthian columns, occasionally glancing up at the wooden platform above the earth bank and stone walls. There was an eerie silence about the town, and they saw and heard no one. Polyamis reached into his sack and pulled out a long wooden needle with a length of twine attached. He set about working free a wooden bolt that held the door shut from within, stabbing and dragging it back bit by bit until it came loose from the bracket that held it. They filed unseen into Calleva and melted into a maze of narrow alleyways between mud brick and thatch cottages that occupied the poorer eastern quarter of the town.

THE FOLLOWING MORNING Marcus lined his troops up on the parade ground and went with Drustan to the entrance of the barracks. They opened wide the wooden gates to see a line of eager-faced villagers and townsfolk, numbering about two hundred. Marcus and his men laughed at the favourable response to the call to arms and ushered them in for assessment.

"Our chief was wise to mention free meals, clothing and a roof over their heads," Marcus joked to a comrade. Some elderly men and women were detailed for weapon-making, cooking and support, with the remainder divided into Decums, or groups of ten, each allocated to one of Marcus's men as their commander. Marcus hoped their numbers would swell over the next few days as word spread around the district of what had transpired. As Marcus briefed his new unit commanders, Drustan came in through the gate, leading a group of shuffling men in chains.

"My lord, these men are deserters who were languishing almost forgotten in the cells. Most are Briton auxiliary, but two are Roman legionaries."

Marcus surveyed the sorry-looking group of a dozen men and said, "I will release you from your chains and your crimes will be forgotten if you fight under my command. Otherwise, I will send you back to rot. What say you?"

The ten Britons conferred in a huddle, but one of the Roman soldiers spoke directly to him: "I am Quintus Brutus and this is Ahmed Salaam; we are foot soldiers of the Fifth Legion, formerly garrisoned in Corinium. We will fight for you."

Marcus was curious and asked, "Tell me, what were your crimes?"

Quintus replied, "We were the only survivors of an ambush of our patrol by renegade Britons as we marched through the forest between Corinium and Aquae Sulis. We could do no more for our comrades and fled into the woods. After some days we were captured by Britons loyal to your garrison commander and handed over for a reward. We cannot go back to our legion, sir, and will gladly fight for your cause."

"You are welcome, Quintus and Ahmed - I will take you at your word, but you must stay close to me." He turned to the group of Britons and in so doing, switched from speaking Latin to the Brythonic spoken by the locals. "And what say you?"

"My lord, we will serve you if you free us," said one.

"What is your name and why were you held prisoner?" Marcus demanded.

"I am Gerulitis, my lord, and we are all of the Icenii people. We were part of a Roman auxiliary cohort and escaped from a battle with sea-borne invaders to the east." He pointed in the direction from where the sun rose, rattling his chains in the process. "Our loyalty to the Romans was weak, my lord, I freely admit, but we will willingly fight for a Briton cause, for your cause."

Marcus knew he would have to keep an eye on them, but also knew they would prove useful as they had undergone military training. "Release them, but under my command, and they must report directly to Drustan here who will separate them and assign them to defence duties."

After the convicts had been unshackled and dispersed, Marcus noticed one group hanging back by the barracks entrance.

"You there, come forward!" he commanded.

As they moved towards him he could see the five men and three women were similarly attired in woollen smocks and leather shoes. The men had three or four days of stubble on their chins and their uncombed hair cut to shoulder length. As they drew near he noticed brands on their inner arms. Polyamis stood before him and raised his head to look Marcus in the eyes. He had been trained not to speak to a Roman citizen until spoken to.

"You have the look of Roman house slaves," Marcus observed, reverting to Latin. "Pray, tell me how you came to slip your masters?"

Polyamis bowed and answered, "My lord, we were house slaves and escaped our masters as they departed in the night. We fled to the woods but have now chosen to return to the town and throw ourselves on your mercy and offer you our services. Five of us would serve as soldiers and three women as kitchen workers."

Marcus and Drustan shared a look and burst out laughing - unusual merriment that drew a few curious glances.

"Well, spirited slave warriors and kitchen wenches, you are most welcome to our army!" Marcus said, slapping Polyamis on the shoulder. "But you are no longer slaves as you have freely chosen to stay and join our cause."

Polyamis and his band grinned at each other at this news.

Marcus eyed the broad-shouldered Camillus and asked, "And where do you hail from, big man?"

Camillus replied, "I am from Nubia, a distant province of Rome, my lord."

"But can you wield a sword?"

"I can, my lord, and throw a javelin far."

Marcus nodded. "Then I will hand you men over to my deputy, Drustan, who will find you uniforms and place you in a unit."

He addressed the women standing at the back of the group. "Those who would serve in our kitchen should present themselves at the mess. You are welcome!"

Marcus had his new defence force, numbering about two hundred, fall into line.

He stood tall as he addressed them, "You are the new cohort of Calleva and will occupy this fort and live like soldiers, away from your families, as you undergo training in weapons and tactics. We will drill you like Roman soldiers and provide uniforms and weapons. A new age is beginning for us Britons and we must take responsibility for our own affairs and fight our own battles. From now on our battle cry will be, 'Viva Valorian! Viva Atrebates!'" They all chanted in response, and any townsfolk outside of their walls must have heard and been comforted. Their conquerors had brought civilisation and organisation to the subdued Britons, putting them ahead of the marauding barbarian tribes who lived beyond the boundaries of their empire. Now they had something worth fighting for, something worth defending.

Chapter Four

ON THE SOUTH coast the victorious Saxon leader, Cerdric, surveyed the smoking ruins of the once busy Roman port. He was one of four powerful Saxon chiefs who had divided up the south and east of Britannia for conquest and plunder before setting off in their longboats from Saxony. Their homeland was under threat from Visigoths pushing hard from the east, and the land itself was flooded and unsuitable for farming after many winters of rain. Surely signs from their gods to seek new lands across the waters.

He sent out scouting groups on foot along the coast and a dozen warriors on captured horses up the Roman road. The riders travelled half the distance to Calleva Atrebatum where they found a staging inn. They slaughtered the few remaining inhabitants, slaked their hunger and thirst and pillaged what they could, returning to report before nightfall. The existence of the Roman town at a four-way crossroads twenty miles further along the road remained unknown to them.

Cerdric stroked his long, plaited, blond beard and muttered, "All roads lead somewhere. Torture the captives until they tell us what lies beyond the inn, and at what distance."

AN ORDERLY CALM had descended on the inhabitants of Calleva Atrebatum as they hustled to prepare for possible attack. The town layout was a rough hexagon, divided into quarters by two main roads that crossed at a public square outside a large forum building that dominated the centre of the town. The Romans had only allowed citizens, soldiers, tradesmen and merchants to live within the walled town that covered an area of one hundred acres. Most townsfolk who were engaged in supported the Roman garrison occupied one crowded quarter in tightly-knit terraced housing with small yards. There was a sewer system, communal fresh water from deep springs, and oil lamp street lighting. The second quarter was taken up by army barracks, the third had villas for wealthy citizens, temples, a bath house, senate and courthouse, and the fourth quarter had a traveller's rest house, taverns, warehousing, livestock pens, workshops and public baths.

It was a perfectly positioned staging post, with roads radiating out to other Roman towns in all four directions. To the east, Londinium; to the north, Dorchester and Corinium; to the west, Aquae Sulis; to the south, Noviomagus and Venta Belgarum. Stone walls six yards high stood on an earth bank encircling the town, with wooden parapets atop, along its entire length, interrupted by stone tower with platforms dominating each bend in the wall, and at the four points of the compass stood fortified stone gatehouses. Surrounding the walled town was a dry ditch, and each gatehouse had a drawbridge to span it.

The Romans had ruthlessly enforced a policy of forbidding the development of shanty dwellings or the growing of crops outside the town walls, for up to one hundred yards in each direction, with the forest bordering on three sides of the clearing and the way open to rolling hills to the south. Farms were located a short cart ride away to the east and west in clearings cut into the mighty and intimidating forest. Marcus was now grateful for this policy of keeping a clear field of vision with no hiding places close to the town's walls.

It had been many years since the drawbridges at the south and north gatehouses had been raised, and this was Marcus's first concern – to secure the gatehouses and test the withering rope mechanisms. He ensured that there were two shifts for each gatehouse, including archers above, and a continuous roster of guards on each of the towers. The east and west gatehouses did not have drawbridges; instead, they were approached directly by stone bridges over the ditch. Marcus hoped that their foes would not notice.

He divided his units between guarding and weapons training and rode out with two comrades to reconnoitre the surrounding area. The land fell away to the south, but there was hilltop five miles on from which they could see the smoke rising from the Halfway House Inn. Saxons, surely. Would they come straight on? He needed to be sure. They rode on cautiously to investigate.

They dismounted before reaching the smouldering ruins of the wooden buildings and crept forward on foot. Apart from starlings tweeting and the snuffling of wild boar foraging, there was quiet. They walked out into the bright sunlight and the boar trotted back to their forest trails. There were six bloody bodies littered around the site. The three soldiers had known some of those unfortunate people. Bitterness filled their hearts as they saw the grievous wounds of the family who had run the Inn, and a pair of luckless travellers.

Nothing remained to be salvaged, and Marcus made the hard decision to leave the bodies where they lay, knowing the Saxons would return and wanting to keep their presence hidden for the time being. This was a stark warning of what to expect from the heartless invaders who would spare no one in their lust for killing and plunder. As they moved to leave, a noise to their left made them grip their sword handles. A boy walked out of the forest and stood, uncertainly, until Marcus waved him to approach.

"Who are you, boy?" Marcus asked.

The forlorn, dirty child spoke in a quiet voice, "Sir, I am Brian, son of the Inn Keeper. My parents lie here, killed by raiders."

"We are sorry for your loss. You must come with us to the safety of the town. These barbarians will return."

"Will you help me bury them?" he asked.

"We cannot. The Saxons will soon be here, and we must not alert them to our presence. I am sorry, Brian, but we will make an offering to the gods in our temple."

The troop rode away in silence, the tearful boy sitting behind Drustan, as crows sat patiently on tree branches and buzzards circled overhead.

Calleva was filling up with farmers from outlying areas, and many flocked to the dowdy wattle and daub Christian church or the classical stone-columned temples to the Roman gods, in particular the god of legionaries, Mithras. Outside, market stalls were doing a good trade in wooden effigies and live chickens for sacrifice, and temple attendants were busy carrying out buckets of blood and entrails. The pagan and Christian priests were working overtime to conduct services and give assurance to their anxious and fearful followers.

Fear and uncertainty played into the hands of the new administration, who busied themselves with preparations for evacuation and defence whilst giving out reassurances they did not feel themselves. Lack of information was a problem, and Valorian sent riders out to other tribal chieftains to exchange news, appeal for assistance to repel the Saxons, and request a meeting to debate their post-Roman defence strategy. Meanwhile, he knew he had a problem with his scheming brother, Vortigern, whom he had sent to bring their father and his household into the town. They had not arrived, and he sent out another rider to find out what was causing the delay.

Marcus reported what he had found at the Inn and gave his opinion that the Saxons would most likely march along the road in the coming days. He would position lookouts along the road from the following day. Back in his barracks, Marcus was pleased to see that more volunteers had come in during the day, swelling their numbers to about three hundred new recruits. Many were farmers with little combat experience. It was no easy thing to kill a man, and he knew the Saxons would be terrifying opponents. An uneasy silence descended over the town that evening, with small groups talking in hushed tones, clustered around simmering cauldrons of broth. The population of the town had grown to over one-and-a-half-thousand men, women and children.

The next day Marcus turned his attention to ways to slow down and degrade their opponents. The Romans had left four catapults, wooden machines capable of flinging large stones over the walls to a distance of up to one hundred paces. He had them positioned behind the south wall and test-fired them to mark the range. He ordered cauldrons of pitch be boiled up and set fire traps outside the south wall. With Valorian's reluctant assent, he travelled south on the road for fifteen miles, to a bridge over a fast-flowing river, with a group of carpenters and tree-fellers. They weakened the central span of the bridge so that it would break under the weight of a heavy load. They set a trap of falling rocks in a ravine through which the road passed, leaving Drustan with three soldiers to wait on either side of high cliffs, ready to manually release rock slides by knocking away wooden props. He would lead a troop of mounted archers who would harass the approaching army over the last five miles. Beyond this, there was little else he could do.

Valorian called him that evening to the Forum for a review of their situation. He walked up the white stone steps, past Corinthian columns, and into the circular marble hall - a miniature representation of imperial Rome already starting to look out of place. Marcus briefed the dozen toga-clad elders of his defensive measures and wondered if they could expect reinforcements. Downcast eyes and shaking of grey heads told him this was unlikely. Furthermore, they would soon be leaving the town and recommended the evacuation of all non-combatants. Valorian reluctantly agreed and reported his concern that his brother, Vortigern, had gone missing, and may have headed south to make a deal with the Saxons.

Marcus spoke with quiet determination. "If this is so, Vortigern's report of our weak and virtually defenceless state may play to our advantage. If they approach with confidence we will strike them hard."

His words did little to sooth the fears of the Fathers, whose brows were wrinkled in deep thought as they shifted uncomfortably on cold marble benches. They were the representatives of local tribal groups and were men of position and wealth with much to lose. It was time to hand over defence of the town to the soldiers, and for them to withdraw to their farmsteads and villas, or quietly into the forest, as their ancestors had done when the Romans first appeared over four hundred years earlier. Marcus added as he left, "A few more men and able-bodied women to man the walls would be welcome."

WORD CAME FROM scouts the next day that the Saxon army was on the march, reaching the burnt out Halfway House. Marcus gave his final instructions to the defence force, leaving Drustan in charge, and rode out with twenty troops including Quintus and Ahmed, armed with bows, arrows, spears and swords. They took up positions on the cliff tops on either side of the narrow gorge, past the point where the rock fall was planned. A scout reported that the central section of the bridge had collapsed under the weight of an ox-drawn cart, swept away down river. The rest of the Saxon army was now camped for the night on the far side of the river as they felled trees to repair the bridge. Marcus ordered his men to make camp, satisfied that they had delayed the advance of their foe by one day. Maybe a Roman legion would come to the aid of the town, although the Second and Fifth Legions, who had garrisoned much of the west, had already passed by months earlier, sparking rumours of a Roman withdrawal. They had not been paid for two months and their own garrison had now gone. They had truly been abandoned.

The drums of the Saxons could be heard the following morning approaching the rocky outcrop, and Quintus led four riders ahead to survey the gorge. They rode up and down, and, satisfied, returned to their leader. Marcus calmed his men ahead of their first engagement with the fearsome Saxons. All were glad for the experience of Quintus and the silent Ahmed, who sharpened and polished his sword. The approaching army narrowed and filed through the gorge, four abreast, led by two drummers banging out a steady march. Marcus had instructed the rock-fall teams to let a dozen through before knocking their wooden struts out, and they proved to be reliable as the rocks cascaded down onto the soldiers below, whose attempts to cover their heads with their wooden shields were to no avail. In the ensuing mayhem below, and billowing dust cloud, Marcus ordered his archers to fire. Arrows rained down on those who had passed ahead of the rock fall, and many were cut down before they could find cover. After another volley of arrows, Marcus ordered his men to mount up and withdraw.

They had seen the size of the Saxon force, about three hundred warriors, almost all on foot. Had more arrived to join them, since the sacking of Noviomagus? Marcus noted there were only about twenty mounted soldiers, before ordering they fall back to the last high hill before the plateau on which their town sat.

He turned to Drustan as they rode side-by-side and said, "We can't make our town invisible, so we're going to have to defend ourselves. If we don't face up to the Saxons, they'll prevail and give no quarter to anyone they find."

Dread drum beats announced the approach of the invaders, a sound intended to strike terror into the hearts of those in their way. Marcus decided he could achieve most by drawing out their few riders and eliminating them.

An ambush was set, and a dozen Saxon riders took the bait, chasing six fleet horsemen into a wooded glade where waiting archers fired on the pursuers. Those brought down were instantly attacked with sword and axe by those hiding in the trees, led with enthusiasm by Quintus and Ahmed, as a mounted skirmish took place between remaining riders of both sides. Marcus felt the thrill of hand-to-hand combat against the physically bigger Saxons for the first time, killing his opponent with a thrust of his Roman lance, and then watched with pride as his men killed the rest. He also noted how the leadership of two experienced legionaries made a marked difference to the confidence of his men in a combat situation. Their weapons were collected and the horses rounded up. Brian, the orphan boy, could now ride his own mount and lead a string of horses. They could do no more that day.

The band of riders entered through the south gatehouse and the drawbridge was pulled up behind them to complete the defensive barrier facing the oncoming barbarian force. Valorian greeted him with a grim face: "Marcus, you are most welcome, but what news of the Saxons?"

Marcus brushed the dust off his epaulettes and looked up to the sky. His eyes fixed on a falcon falling out of the sun, gaining in speed until it smashed into a wood pigeon, stunning it and sending it spinning to the ground. Valorian had followed his gaze.

"Nature is cruel," Marcus said. "The predator will stalk and kill his quarry without feeling. His very survival depends on it. It is only Man who takes pleasure from the kill. The Saxons will be here by nightfall, three hundred strong, and should they breach our walls, they will spare no one."

Abandoned

Chapter Five

MARCUS ORGANISED HIS sub-commanders to man the defences and then went to visit his family in their new home, the villa of the former Roman garrison commander. As he made his way there, along streets of frightened people, he noticed that fewer were clothed in the Roman fashion, and more in cured leather and animal skins in the tradition of the local Atrebates tribe. Calleva had been an important town at a major crossroads that had become prosperous on trade over the past four hundred mainly peaceful years. Their lives and very existence was now at a crossroads. He hurried through the fretful crowds to his waiting wife, children and mother.

Marcus kissed his wife, Cordelia, and patted her pregnant belly.

"And what shall we call our child?" he asked her.

"Your mother has a strong feeling it will be a boy and wishes to call him 'Uther' after a Briton tribal leader from the distant past," she replied.

"Is that so?" Marcus said with a smile. "And what if it's a girl?"

They both laughed.

Marcus kissed her forehead and asked, "Where is my mother?"

"Morcant is in the temple of the Druids, making sacrifice," she replied, shaking her head to chase her long chestnut braids to her back.

Marcus poured them both some water from a pewter jug and said, "I'll go to fetch her. Now you must make ready to leave. I will arrange for a horse and cart to take you north, to your father's house. He will keep you safe. We must prepare for the worst. The Saxons will soon be upon us with terrible force."

She could see the strain on the face of her young warrior husband. "Marcus, you must come with us and leave this place!" she pleaded. "The Romans have abandoned us, and we cannot hope to fight an army of Saxons with just a handful of warriors and farmers' boys. It's hopeless!"

Marcus held her close and kissed the top of her head, smelling the sweet scent of rose petals. "It is not hopeless. We have a chance of defending this town, and I must do all I can. All my training as a Roman officer has been for this moment, and I will not fail. My love, you and my mother must go. I will join you or send word once we have defeated these wild men from across the waters. Go now and make ready." He gave instructions to their house slaves, took what he needed for himself and went in search of his mother.

He had a feeling he would find her in the hall of the tribal leader, now used as a temple by the Druids who had suddenly appeared from their groves in the forest. It was tucked away behind rows of roughly-thatched mud brick and wooden houses in the poorest quarter of the town, the stronghold of the Atrebates tribe. He pushed past crowds blocking the entrance into the high beamed hall, his eyes slowly adjusting to the gloom, conscious that no one was dressed in the Roman fashion.

In the centre stood a druid clad in a long grey woven gown tied at the waist, with a flowing white beard and a crown of holly vine bright with red berries. He held a wooden staff and was preaching in a loud voice, in the language of the tribe, to a room full of silent, expectant people. Marcus peered through the gloom and saw his mother kneeling beside the altar, her hands red with blood, holding a knife, next to a basket of slaughtered fowl. Marcus moved to one side, conspicuous in his Roman officer's uniform, and listened.

"...our ancestors are calling us to return to the old ways. The Men of Rome have gone, returning to their homeland. We should remember that our forefathers fought them for this land and were defeated in battle and forced into slavery under Roman rule. But we have outlasted them, and can now celebrate our freedom and return to the ways of our ancestors..."

"What freedom do we have when the Saxons are at our gates?" Marcus shouted, breaking the hypnotic mood that surrounded the holy man from the woods. They turned and looked at him, some with hatred in their eyes.

The Druid pointed at Marcus with his staff: "Look at the puppet of the Romans! He wears their clothes and has their manners. He will lead you all to your deaths! The Saxons will soon go back to the sea. Flee to the woods and wait!"

Marcus was surrounded by a pushing mob, chanting, "No more Rome!" As he backed towards the shaft of sunlight stabbing through a high opening, he made an appeal for support: "Friends! I have Atrebates blood in my veins, like you! The Romans have gone, but we must come together to defend ourselves and our town! Let us not lose what the Romans gave us. It is ours now!"

A woman's shrill voice cut through the stifling atmosphere: "Listen to my son! He has the knowledge of the Romans and the heart of a Briton! He is of my bloodline and is our only hope. Follow him, those who can fight! The others can flee to the woods, knowing that our brave men and women have stayed to fight the Saxons, who are but mortals, though they hunt and kill without mercy. The runes speak only of fire and murder. We must resist or die as sheep tethered to a stake!"

Her words hit home at the fearful group of wretched townsfolk, who had turned to the Druid in this makeshift temple for comfort and guidance, now looked about with torn expressions.

The Druid raised his staff and shouted above the murmuring, "Do not listen to her! She has lain with a Roman soldier and given birth to this half-breed who stands before you! Turn away from them and follow me now to the woods! Our cousins to the North, the Dobunni, will give us shelter. Those who remain here will die!"

Marcus puffed out his chest and stood tall and straight, "...and follow me, those who will fight for their town, families and their livelihood!" Two young boys ran to Marcus as adults dithered. "Will you let children fight for you?" Marcus challenged the room. This had some effect as a dozen adults drifted towards him. Many more flocked to the Druid and were led away through an opening at the back of the long building. Morcant came towards him and embraced him warmly. She smelled of chicken blood and had offal in her hair.

"My son! Your day of destiny has come! I dreamt you were riding into battle on the back of a fire-breathing dragon, its wings spread wide as it took to the skies. You must wear this charm to keep you safe." She tied a strip of leather around his neck from which hung a circular bronze medallion with a dragon etched on, bearing a small green stone for its eye. He received it with pride, well aware that his mother came from a line of sorceresses with healing powers and the ability to conjure visions of the future. He asked her to return with him to the villa so she could prepare to leave with Cordelia and the rest of their household for a place of safety.

Marcus helped his wife and mother pack their things onto a cart and charged his two servants to take good care of them. His mother appeared at his side, holding a woollen tunic. It was grey in colour but with a hand-embroidered flying dragon on the front. Clearly, the old woman had spent time in making it, as the collar of the tunic was embroidered in fine gold thread.

"Thank you, my mother, you and the gods honour me," Marcus said, receiving it and pulling it over the top of his tunic. He had already decided that he would not let his soldiers see him wearing such a thing and would remove it once she was gone. He was touched by the gesture and knew, as his family prepared to depart, that he had something of great value worth fighting for.

Morcant had the final words: "My son, I believe your spirit is closely bound with the clever and powerful dragon, whom some say are mystical creatures of our imagination. But I tell you that dragons are real creatures that live far away to the west in mountain caves and deep pools, rarely seen by the people of these lands, except when they fly across the sky in a trail of fire! Henceforth your name shall be Marcus Pendragon, and the dragon's spirit will guide you to achieve your heart's desire!"

IN THE BARRACKS those soldiers not on defence duties began to prepare themselves for the battle ahead. Polyamis gathered up his followers and they went to make offerings.

"The Temple of Fortuna is close by," he said, taking Prisca's hand and leading his band of former slaves, now attired as soldiers and kitchen workers. The five men wore copper forearm guards that covered their slave brands, and the women wore long-sleeved tunics.

"Fortuna will bring us luck in the coming defence of our town," Januarius said, dodging a donkey cart of apples driven by an old man. He helped himself from the back of the cart and bit a large mouthful of the sweet fruit, tossing another one to a grateful Camillus.

"Should you not be making an offering of that fruit to the goddess," Prisca chided.

"We shall pool our coin and buy some fowl to offer," Polyamis said.

They had arrived at a stone-fronted temple, outside of which a cluster of noisy traders vied for custom from the many worshippers who had come to make sacrifice. Polyamis collected enough for two chickens and walked inside, holding the squawking birds by their feet.

"I would like to eat this one; my stomach is rumbling," Camillus whispered.

Polyamis ignored his burly friend, who caught the eye of everyone he passed. He chose a wizened priestess from a line, attracted by her cloak of green wool with pinned feathers and golden edging.

Bowing low, he said, "Priestess of Fortuna, sacred goddess of good fortune and slaves, we wish to pay homage and would make a sacrifice for our own good luck in the defence of our town from barbarian raiders. Will you make our sacrifice and importune the goddess to watch over us?"

The grey-haired woman eyed them to get their measure, noting each had covered their forearms. "I will make your sacrifice to the goddess, for she smiles on those who are humble enough to ask for her grace and looks with favour on... slaves."

Prisca's eyes widened and she glanced at her covered forearm.

The priestess picked up a small basket and motioned Polyamis and Camillus, who held the flapping chickens, to follow her into a courtyard, to an altar with a wooden base and polished marble slab atop. A bronze cast of the goddess, her hair flowing as she rode in a chariot, was flanked by pewter vases vibrant with fresh cut flowers. Other groups of worshippers clustered around similar altars arranged at equal distances around the edges of the open space.

The priestess took a pewter chalice from her basket and set it on the altar; she waited until Polyamis had dropped some coin into the basket and then nodded her thanks. Drawing a dagger from under her robes, with practised cuts to their throats, she silenced the struggling fowl. Polyamis and Camillus dribbled chicken blood into the chalice, and the scrawny corpses were soon added to the pile of offerings stinking before the marble plinth.

Raising the chalice to the skies, their celebrant mumbled a supplication and then drank from the cup. Each of the eight was offered the cup and sipped the warm blood, or went through the motion of it, before they all stood solemn-faced at the altar and repeated the words of the priestess's chant:

"Oh, mighty Fortuna, goddess of prosperity and good chance, save us from ruin and death in these troubled times! Watch over these brave men as they prepare for battle. Hail Fortuna!"

Prisca looked into the white clouds floating to the skies, straining her eyes to see the chariot, the flowing hair, and then sighed. Why could she not see the goddess, here in Fortuna's own temple, at a time when her heart brimmed with gratitude for her freedom and the safety that had so far been granted to Polyamis, that bold man of hers?

As they left, a thoughtful Polyamis took Camillus and Prisca to one side and said in a hushed tone, "You are my only friends in this world, and I wish you both safety and good fortune in what may lie ahead." He looked over his shoulder before he continued, speaking quickly with his head down. "I must tell you both that I buried some treasures stolen from my master in a pit under his house, beneath a reed mat. There lies coin, jewellery and a bronze eagle. Should I fall in battle, and you both survive, I wish you to recover those items and use them to make better lives for yourselves."

Prisca frowned and gripped his arm. "Do not talk of your own death, Polyamis. The goddess will protect us and we shall all have good lives as free men and women."

Camillus placed his large hand on Polyamis's shoulder. "My friend, Poly-anus, I shall watch over you in the battle ahead, and we shall all live to see the benefits of your treasure. It will only be a matter of days before we sweep out this plague of Saxons."

Chapter Six

VALORIAN WAS PLEASED to see Marcus back by his side. They could now hear the war trumpets and drum beats of the Saxons approaching from the south. Scout riders came swiftly as the drawbridge was finally pulled up and secured. Archers and javelin throwers lined the walls as they waited for the first sight of their foe.

"You must now take charge of the south wall defences," Valorian commanded. "We have evacuated half of the town through the north gate, and it gives us some comfort to know our families and friends will be safe. We have no news of relief from any quarter, and therefore must look to our own resources. I will remain with you to meet our enemy and have detailed my guard to act as a rapid deployment force in case of surprise attacks on the other gates. Our towers will be our eyes. Good luck to you all!"

Cerdric and his men marched over the last hill and lined up facing the south gate. Marcus counted two ranks, each of about a hundred and fifty men. They would be no match for a Roman cohort but were a fearsome foe for their lightly armed and largely inexperienced defensive force. A small group of riders detached themselves and came forward. When they were barely one hundred yards away, Valorian froze. Marcus followed his stare to a small group of Britons on horseback with the Saxon leaders, one of whom was Valorian's treacherous younger brother, Vortigern. The dozen riders came forward, close to the gatehouse, and the two brothers faced each other.

"Your brother's treachery may be our undoing," Marcus said to his mortified leader.

"He knows our weaknesses and must surely exploit them." Valorian spoke with bitterness in his voice, knowing that much suffering would be the result of his brother's move to help the enemy.

"He means to kill me and become Chief, and perhaps a King under the rule of Saxons. It is a bitter prospect for our brave people, who will come to realise that the Romans were fairer masters than these brutes."

Their leader was a big man with a long, plaited beard tied in three places, flowing from a broad, weather-beaten warrior's face, beneath a horned helmet. He oozed confidence and menace.

"I am Cerdric, come with my three brothers-in-arms to take this island of Britannia. I am your new lord, and demand you open your gates, so my army may enter and see your Roman treasures and enjoy your ale and women-folk!" He turned to share the joke with his deputies, and the three traitors in their group.

Marcus grimaced, able to grasp his meaning as he spoke in a Celtic language similar to that of the Atrebates tribe.

Cerdric turned back to face Marcus and Valorian and thundered, "To whom do I speak?"

Valorian spoke quietly to Marcus: "I will address my comments to my brother before acknowledging that barbarian." He stepped forward and placed his hands on the wooden parapet, looking down at Vortigern and his treacherous companions.

"It grieves me to see my own brother, son of noble chief, Tincomarus, keeping such poor company. All hail Vortigern, traitor and lackey of a barbarian invader! You have brought these thieves and murderers to our gates, but you see they are barred, and our walls defended by stout-hearted Britons, whose resolve is stiffened by the sight of you. Shame on you! You will die a traitor to your family and your people!"

A loud cheer went up from those manning the walls as they waved their weapons at the enemy and bellowed their defiance. Marcus was pleased to see their bravado. It would help to give them courage for the bitter and brutal fighting that was to come.

Cerdric laughed and shouted above the din, "This family reunion is touching, but you must know, Valorian, that your brother has told us of your weaknesses and the small number of men at your disposal. I can even see that you have recruited women to do your fighting!" He laughed and pointed his battle axe in the direction of a young woman holding a bow on the battlements. In her anger she placed an arrow and drew her bow, aiming at the Saxon chief.

"You make a big target, my lord," she shouted. Her comrades banged their swords and spears against their shields in a show of support. Valorian waved at her to put her bow down.

Marcus turned to him and said in a whisper, "My lord, her show of defiance gives me an idea. We owe these villains no respect. We could cut their leaders down right now, along with your brother, and leave the snake headless." Valorian studied him. They both knew their position was weak and the Saxons would most likely make short work of them.

"We want nothing from them except for them to leave, or die on the tips of our lances," Marcus added.

"Very well. Get your best archers ready. When I finish speaking, fire on them." He turned back to the smug Saxon leader: "Mighty Cerdric, I can see the power of your army and know that my brother's knowledge can give you an added advantage. But know this. We are not of a mind to surrender to you meekly. Your wicked brutality in laying waste our neighbour's port is known to us, and we would expect only death and destruction, as that is your way. I say to you that I am Valorian, true heir to my father's lands, and you shall not enter!"

With that he took a step back and Marcus, along with a dozen archers, stepped forward and aimed their arrows at the group of startled horsemen. The arrows flew and hit their marks, three riders falling to the ground, horses rearing and bolting, some with arrows in their flanks. Cerdric, taking an arrow in his thigh, spun his horse around and dug his heels into its flank, urging it forward into a gallop. A second hail of arrows fell on the group, and one from the female warrior landed in the black bearskin on Cerdric's back, penetrating far enough to make him wriggle in pain.

"My brother is down!" Valorian said, pointing to a struggling man on the ground.

"Shall we finish him, my lord, or send out a squad to grab the wounded?" Marcus asked, as a third volley of arrows fell on those who were crawling.

"Yes! Get him and bring him in!" Valorian commanded. Marcus ordered a halt, threw down his bow and rushed down the steps, shouting at the gatekeepers to open one side. He rushed out with half a dozen soldiers and grabbed the two wounded survivors, one Saxon and one Briton, and dragged them inside. Four bodies remained outside, and Cerdric and his surviving guards had by now re-joined his army, who shouted and waved their axes and swords at the Roman town walls in anger. Morale was high on the ramparts as the Britons shouted curses at the two dead traitors - Vortigern's guards had been notorious bullies well known to them.

Vortigern was not so talkative now, cowering forlornly before his elder brother's withering gaze. "Take him to my villa and treat his wounds," Valorian ordered, "but keep him under close guard. I will speak with him later. And put this other wretch in chains." He returned with Marcus to the ramparts above the gate, eager to see what the Saxons would do.

"They are angry, my lord!" Marcus laughed. Cerdric must have instructed his deputies to advance, as a steady drum beat and blast of trumpets announced their forward movement. The Saxons, banged their swords and axes on their shields in time to the drums and marched in a steady line towards the South Wall, chanting a low, guttural war cry.

"Make ready the catapults!" Marcus shouted. There was a flurry of activity and rocks tied in animal skins and soaked in pitch were loaded into the cradles of the four wooden machines. Men with burning torches stood by, waiting for his command. Marcus looked out for the painted stone markers as the Saxons approached in two long lines. They had set some traps at sixty yards from the walls, holes filled with sharp objects and covered with turf, and some fire traps with strips of pitch designed to ignite on impact from burning catapult fire or flaming arrows. Practice sessions had taken place in the previous days that had given some much-needed belief to the apprehensive defence force. Marcus could see poorly equipped men and women, untrained and inexperienced in combat, lined up along the ramparts, conversing nervously to encourage each other and allay their fears.

They should be fearful, Marcus thought, and he was glad they had not yet witnessed the brutality and utter ruthlessness of these flaxen-haired devils from across the sea. Their contempt for the lives of all peoples not of their kind was terrifying to behold, as he and his men had witnessed during the sacking of their nearest port town. This will not end well. The high-handed Romans had gone, and left them to their fate, but Marcus was half Roman, and understood the benefits of an ordered and organised community. It was now his responsibility to protect his people within this Roman town, built on the site of their tribal citadel, from the dreaded Saxons outside.

"We will greet them with fire and cause mayhem in their ranks, from which our archers should profit," he shouted above the din at an anxious Valorian. Marcus raised his hand and held it high, waiting for the front line of the Saxons to pass the coloured stones and lines of pitch hidden under sods of dry grass.

"Light them!" he instructed the torch-bearers. "Fire!" he shouted and the four catapults let fly with their burning missiles arcing high over the walls. "Reload!" he shouted whilst they were still airborne. The balls crashed into the enemy, black smoke trailing in their wake. The Saxons scattered in fear and panic, the grass around their feet catching fire as they ran away from comrades who had been ignited. Some then stumbled into hidden holes, breaking their ankles and lacerating themselves on sharp stones wedged there for that purpose.

"Fire!" Marcus instructed the archers, and arrows rained down on the disorganised rabble, hitting home as few held their shields up. Marcus instructed them to continue firing their arrows and only stop when his cavalry was out of the gate. He ran down the steps and leapt onto his horse, drawing his sword and rallying his thirty mounted troops. Half were relatively new recruits who had not tasted battle before.

"Have no fear in your hearts! We must kill or be killed! Viva Valorian! Viva Atrebates!"

They took up the cry as he took his lance from his squire and shouted, "Open the gates!"

He led the charge across the wooden bridge over the muddy moat; clattering into the scrambled shield wall of Saxons; stabbing with his lance and slashing with his sword. Valorian rallied a squad of one hundred-foot soldiers, a second wave, who ran out to join the fray as the final throw of the dice for the thinly-stretched defenders.

The leaderless Saxons looked about for instructions as they were pushed back towards the burning patches of ground, finally breaking and running through the gaps between the flames in disarray, leaving a third of their force behind lying dead or wounded.

Marcus called his men back from chasing the fleeing enemy and returned to the safety of the fortified town. It was a war of attrition and numbers mattered. He knew they had inflicted a serious defeat on their foe, perhaps enough to make them consider withdrawing. His own force had suffered few casualties, and his new recruits had been successfully blooded.

Their herbal dispensary had grown into a temporary hospital, with about a dozen wounded now being treated. Marcus detailed Drustan to made sure enough guards were in position in the towers and on the walls, with instructions for a messenger to be sent to his quarters every hour to report on the movement or non-movement of the Saxons. Evening descended and the Saxons lit camp fires on a ridge about two hundred yards away.

The sun went down on the dead lying strewn across the meadow between the town and the Saxon camp, with crows and ravens squabbling over their remains. Marcus's thoughts turned to his absent family. Had they reached the safety of his wife's family farmstead? He hoped they would not have cause to man their defences at that place.

The wounded Saxon warlord, Cerdric, bellowed his displeasure at his entourage. They had suffered an unexpected and costly set back, losing close to one hundred men, a third of their force. Half of their riders were dead, along with their treacherous allies, so they were without intelligence of the layout of their enemy's defences. He rued his complacent approach to their gates and admired the ruthless qualities of his opponents. Cerdric called his son and trusted deputies to his tent and briefed them from his hastily-made bed of twigs and leaves.

"You will travel around their town, staying out of range of archers, and study their defences, looking for points of entry and any signs of weakness where we could more easily breach their walls. Count the men on their walls and towers. Go now!" They hurried out and he succumbed to treatment from his healer who had mixed a potion using dried herbs, dressing his wounds. He had many battle scars and would soon be back on his feet; rest for this patient would be difficult for the herbalist to enforce.

The sentries reported movement of Saxon riders around the perimeter of the town, examining their defences, reminding the anxious Britons that it was far from over. Marcus was walking a complete circuit of the defensive wall, following the Saxon riders, accompanied by his new Roman colleagues.

"Tell me, Quintus, where were you stationed and what battles have you fought?"

"Sir, we were stationed this past year at Corinium with the Fifth Legion, patrolling the western edges of the known world of this once mighty empire of Rome. This past year my section was stationed at a fortress on the western-most outpost, at Isca Augusta, where we fought with wild tribes of fierce Celts. They were painted blue and howled like demons as they came from the woods. We repelled invaders from the sea, who called themselves the Scotti, from the island of Hibernia, to the west where the sun sets. Before that, we came to Britannia with our legion from Gaul, where we fought and won a mighty battle against the combined tribes of that country."

Marcus listened whilst studying the slow movement of three Saxon riders close to the line of trees. "What do you know of the Roman Legions leaving this country?"

"Sir, I overheard my Centurion briefing my cohort commander to prepare us to leave and march to an eastern sea port, where we would be taken by galley to Gaul. There was talk in the mess of barbarian armies attacking in great numbers from the east, and even threatening Rome itself. We had an idea that we would soon be withdrawing from this province, which itself is under attack from north, east and west."

"And now the south," Marcus added. "These coarse barbarians are coming from all sides to rape and pillage. They seem only interested in killing, destruction and profit. There is no bargaining with these people. Maybe it will be the end of Rome if there is a limitless wave of barbarians living beyond the boundaries of the Empire, envious and greedy, with murderous intent."

He instructed torches and braziers be lit around the walls as night fell on the pensive town.

Chapter Seven

THE GREY CLOUDS hung low as dawn crept slowly from the dark forest to the east over the town of Calleva Atrebatum. Marcus and his trusted deputy Drustan ensured that the defensive force of town people, farmers, guards and a few auxiliary cavalry troops, all got a few hours rest. Some had been making offerings to their gods in the pagan temples or Christian church. Whose god would save them from slaughter by the barbarian hordes at their gates? Religious leaders were never more popular than during a crisis. Drustan sent runners around the various temples and through the narrow streets of crowded houses, calling for all those with defensive duties to fall in at first light. There was stirring in the Saxon camp as the smell of scorched animal flesh from their fires carried to the walls.

Valorian joined Marcus at the South gatehouse as the first glow of dawn flickered beyond the dark forest. "What plans do you have for us, Marcus?" he asked of his commander.

"My lord, I feel we should wait to see what they do next. With luck, their leader will not recover from his wounds, and perhaps they will depart. We have a slight advantage in numbers now, after our victory yesterday. But we would be no match for them in a fight. Let us be ready to divide our force if they do the same." He beckoned two men to them. "I have found these two Roman legionaries from the town cells. Deserters they may be, but they have pledged their swords to our cause. This is Quintus, and the other, Ahmed."

Valorian greeted them by grasping forearms, in the Roman manner.

"You are welcome and have this chance to redeem yourselves in battle."

They stood to attention and gave him a Roman salute: clenched fists beating their chests in a firm show of allegiance. Valorian's smile conveyed a feeling of comfort at the sight of trained Romans in his ranks.

"We need four gate commanders in case the enemy attack from four sides. I propose you, my lord, take the North Gate with your guard. Quintus the East and Ahmed the West. Their military experience will greatly aid our defence. Drustan will remain with a small cavalry unit and supervise the catapult team. This is my plan in anticipation of an attempt by the Saxons to probe for areas of weakness around our town." The four men looked at their commander, seeing his confidence and resolve was strong.

Valorian nodded his agreement and descended the steps to his horse and escort. They rode slowly along the main road from south to north, past wooden barricades whilst encouraging the townsfolk to cheer their support. No sooner had Marcus turned his attention to the Saxon camp than he noticed signs of movement there. Were they preparing for attack or withdrawal?

He soon had his answer as their war drums started up a steady beat and the Saxons divided into two groups. Marcus called on his trumpeters to sound the alarm. The defenders scurried to their positions, as the split force marched off around the town, about a hundred men headed to the east and a further hundred headed to the west.

"Prepare to defend the east and west gates!" Marcus yelled. "Drustan! Deploy the catapult crews to east and west! Give the order to fire when they are within range!" Teams of horses were yoked to the heavy catapults amidst much yelling and running about. Marcus ran to the south east tower and climbed up to see the advance of the east Saxon group. Their drummers beat out a steady rhythm as they marched around the edge of the wooded clearing, out of range of their archers. He ordered all his archers on the south wall to divide evenly to east and west.

The Saxons lined-up facing both east and west gates, preparing for an attack. They beat their shields and shouted in time to the drum beats, and slowly began marching towards the gates, carrying a battering ram. It was made of three tree trunks lashed together, Marcus noticed. He glanced across town to the west gate where there was a commotion. They must be employing the same tactics over there. He hoped Ahmed would find his voice and lead with authority.

"Archers, prepare to fire!" he shouted, as the Saxons advanced on the east gate. With a cry of aggression, they broke into a run and bunched together as they made for the gatehouse, over the stone bridge, wooden battering ram to the fore. Each man holding the battering ram was accompanied by a man holding a shield above their heads. A volley of arrows rained on their shields as they got close. Marcus left the tower and ran to the east gatehouse to join Quintus. He had ordered rocks be thrown down on the screaming Saxon hoard as they thudded noisily into the gate.

"Hold steady! Throw your javelins!" Quintus shouted, as arrows, javelins and rocks rained down on the determined enemy. He was a legion javelin champion and picked out a target below to throw at. Marcus joined him with a look of concern as the second loud thud made the gate shake.

"We must stop them ramming the gate; it will not take much more!"

"What do you suggest, sir?" Quintus asked.

"Oil and molasses. Bring oil and molasses!" he shouted, sending several men scurrying. "We must use fire to discourage them." Their arrows and spears were causing minimal attrition to the attackers, who expertly protected their bodies and helmeted heads with round wooded shields ringed with iron bands to prevent them from shattering. With a cry one warrior was speared and fell into the mud at the bottom of the ditch. Hardly a moat, but a deterrent to assault on the walls. A dozen men and women carried large pots filled with dark brown liquid to the top of the gatehouse.

"Quintus! Prepare some archers with flaming arrows. We will pour the oil and molasses on them when they next hit the gate." The thick liquids were poured onto the battering ram team, some smaller pots were thrown, and flaming arrows fired onto them once they had pulled away from the gate. With a cheer from the walls, the men and tree trunk were set alight, causing panic as they dropped it and fled. Archers picked off a number of men as they ran in disarray. Their celebrations were cut short by cries and the sound of fighting coming from the west gate. It had been breached! Marcus barked an order for men to quell the fire outside the gate, and delegated command to a junior. He instructed Quintus and half of the force to follow him. They jumped on waiting horses and galloped across town, followed by running soldiers, rounding the fountain in the central square, passing frightened women, and scattering clucking and quacking fowl.

Fierce fighting met them and they charged into the melee, slashing swords to left and right. Quintus found his comrade, Ahmed, and dismounted to stand side by side, as they fought for their lives. Drustan's blood splattered face managed a grin as Marcus joined him and the rest of his auxiliary cavalry. Fighting had fanned out from the shattered gates into the open area inside the gatehouse. Marcus knew if they could overcome this group of Saxons, before their other force was able to join them, they had a chance of victory. The fighting was bitter and gruesome, as Saxon battle axes rained down mercilessly on the heads of the plucky defenders. The dead and dying littered the ground as both sides continued to hack and slash at each other. Marcus and Drustan urged their horses into the thickest of the fighting with their battle cry 'Viva Atrebates!' taken up by their followers.

Just then, as the battle was in stalemate, Valorian arrived with his guard of twelve riders and they joined in the fray, driving the Saxons back towards the gate, until finally they broke and ran out, with the cries of the Britons ringing in the air. Marcus and Drustan rallied the remaining riders and they followed the Saxons out, cutting down as many as they could outside the walls. Marcus called his riders back to the town, and the battered gates were barricaded up as well as possible. With the cries of victory ringing in his ears and a smirk on his face, Marcus rode back to the east gate in time to see the Saxons making their way back to their camp to the south. Cheers from the defenders sent them on their way. They had survived the double assault. Would there be another?

Marcus, Valorian, Quintus, Ahmed and Drustan met at the south gatehouse to survey their enemy's camp and discuss their next move.

"My lord," Marcus said to Valorian, "we must be prepared for another attack, perhaps even tonight. They are not showing signs of leaving."

"They have barely one hundred and fifty men remaining," Valorian said. "Surely they will give up?"

Marcus stared out to their camp fires, two hundred yards away. "They will not go whilst their leader is alive and urging them to attack. I fear this is not over yet, although the odds are now in our favour. That gives us the option of meeting them in battle. What do you say, Quintus?"

The grizzled veteran grinned. "My lord, they are stronger and more experienced fighters than our willing army of farmers and traders. We should avoid a fight in the open at all costs. But we may be able to pick some of them off with a horseback raiding party."

"My thoughts also, my lord," Drustan said. "We could fire arrows at them and then retreat, to further diminish their force."

Valorian was against the idea. "I feel we should defend the town. So far, we have had the better of things, and may have taken out some of their leaders. Let us stay put. What say you, Marcus?"

They all looked at the thoughtful commander, whose authority they all respected. "They have but few horses, so would be unable to pursue our riders with force. I think a small group of cavalry, perhaps twenty riders, led by Quintus and Drustan. We would not want them to be too comfortable sitting on our meadow!"

Valorian could see the four soldiers were keen on a mission and acquiesced to the proposal. "Alright, but volunteers only, and Marcus must remain here. No undue risks to be taken. You may have your raid."

They agreed to wait until sundown, so the afternoon was taken up with eating, resting and preparations. Marcus walked purposefully to the garrison commanders' office and searched amongst his papers. Before long he found what he was looking for and went to seek out Valorian, carrying a rolled-up parchment map. He found his leader in the Forum at the centre of the town. Marcus accepted a goblet of ale and slaked his thirst. When he saw food spread on a table, he suddenly realised how hungry he was, and piled up a plate. He ate quickly, like a soldier in the field, and then pressed his host to listen to his proposal.

"My lord, there is a settlement of particular interest to us. I believe there are retired legionaries and their families there." He pointed to a village indicated on the map, approximately half way between their position and Aquae Sulis. "I could ride there in barely two hours, my lord, and seek reinforcements to help us."

Valorian looked closely at the parchment with a furrowed brow. "Perhaps some extra men could be found there and persuaded to come, but we need you here, Marcus, to lead our defence force. The men may lose heart if you leave us."

"The raiding party will provide a distraction, and by the time they return it will be night. I should also be back during the night, if unsuccessful. If I am not back during the night, expect me with reinforcements in the morning. I know this place and am confident I can use my rank to persuade them to help us."

"Maybe we have reduced our enemy's ability to overcome us and they will leave?"

Marcus quickly replied, "No, my lord. They will surely attack us again. Most likely, in the morning. They will target one gate, probably the damaged east gate, and attack with all their might. Quintus and Drustan will harry them from behind this evening, which will discourage them from trying a night attack. If I can bring new recruits, we can inflict a final defeat on them. This is the only way we can be safe, my lord."

Valorian rolled his eyes to the ceiling and dwelt on a finely painted mural. A hunter chasing a deer through a forest. He popped a grape into his mouth. "Very well, go quickly and quietly, and try to keep your mission a secret, although you must brief your trusted deputies first. Our very existence is in the balance." He turned to Marcus in desperation, gripping his forearm. "I fear the gods have abandoned us, along with the Romans," he wailed.

"The old gods of our people will protect and guide us. The gods of the Romans may have left with them, but the old deities of the trees, earth and sky still watch over us, my lord. Let me make haste."

Chapter Eight

MARCUS RODE AWAY through the north gate, taking only a young soldier from his auxiliary and his squire as travelling companions. They were soon out of sight of Valorian, who shouted a few instructions at those manning the north gate to snap them out of their sullenness and bade them not to spread the word of Marcus's departure. Drustan and Quintus led their raiding party out of the east gate and circled around behind the Saxons, following a track through the forest known to the auxiliary.

The raiding party dismounted in the trees and crept forward to bushes close by the rear of the Saxon camp. The harsh, guttural language of their enemy could now be heard. It was bitter in tone, with no laughter. They had suffered a defeat and it hurt. They had lost another fifty men in the day's action, leaving them with half of their original number. Still a dangerous force, and there was nothing to suggest to Drustan and Quintus they were thinking of leaving.

They would have time for two volleys of arrow fire, and then they would run for their horses and retread their steps back to the east gate. The sun had gone down and the moon was rising to throw some soft light on the camp, adding to the glow from a dozen fires. The Saxons had built a makeshift village of wood and grass huts. Quintus whispered to Drustan that they should burn the huts. He grinned and produced his tinder pouch. They huddled and agreed a plan of action.

The raiders prepared their arrows and started a fire; each lit the rags bound tightly around the ends of their arrows and fired at the huts, hitting six and lighting them up. In panic and rage, the Saxons hopelessly blundered into the darkness at the edge of the forest, from where their hidden enemy could see them clearly outlined against the backdrop of burning huts. It made the invaders sitting targets and they fired at them, striking a dozen men. Point made, they led their horses into the cover of the dark forest, where they periodically moved position and fired arrows into the angry Saxons' camp. The enemy would not sleep much that night.

THE FORBIDDING FOREST crowded in on Marcus and his two companions as they headed west on the Portway, the echo of their horses' hooves and the screech of an owl the only sounds. There might be bandits, and they stayed alert for any signs of movement, pulling up suddenly when a wild boar broke cover and ran across their path. Pale moonlight lit their long straight path, and Marcus counted the mille-passus marker stones for the next two hours, before judging their position to be close to their goal. His nostrils twitched at the aroma of burning birch wood and he could make out a thin, wispy trail of smoke rising above the trees to their right.

They turned off on a track as a clearing opened up. Marcus knew they were close to a settlement as the track was graded and bordered with drainage ruts. They approached a guard hut with a fire burning in a brazier, and two red-cloaked soldiers challenged them, pointing long lances at the riders.

"Who goes there?" demanded one of the guards.

"Hail, friend. I am Marcus Aquilius, commander of the garrison at Calleva Atrebatum. We have come to speak with your commander."

A GREY DAWN broke on the clearing in which sat the lonely, abandoned fortified town of Calleva Atrebatum. Valorian looked out at the Saxon camp, watching them prepare; for what? Were they leaving or planning another assault? Their anger would be smouldering, along with the ruins of their huts. The night-raid had lifted the morale of the defence force, but they would now have to prepare to rebuff a possible attack without their inspirational and fearless commander, Marcus.

Valorian called his commanders to him. He eyed the pair of Roman legion deserters, broad-shouldered Quintus and the silent Ahmed, and the short, stout auxiliary cavalry deputy commander, Drustan; all had been left behind when the Romans marched out. Proud and defiant in their torn and tattered uniforms, dented helmets tucked under their arms, they awaited Valorian's briefing. He knew not what he wanted to say and was most relieved to be interrupted.

"My lord!" a gate guard puffed. "The warlord is mounting his horse!"

They all squinted across the two hundred yards to the Saxon camp and saw a huge man in a bear fur and horned helmet being pushed up onto a grey horse.

"It must surely be Cerdric," Valorian groaned. "This does not bode well."

The Saxon soldiers formed up behind their leader and a drum beat started. Quintus stepped up to his elbow. "My lord, they are making to move around to the east. I fear they will attack again where we are weakest – at our shattered and barricaded east gate. Send me there to prepare our defences!"

"Go!" Valorian ordered. "And take your silent friend with you. Concentrate our force there. Drustan, move those catapults from the west gate to the east." They hurried off, leaving him to gaze forlornly at the line of Saxon warriors marching around the edge of the clearing in time to an unnerving and steady beat. Their giant leader would surely lead them in one final do-or-die assault. How he wished Marcus was here.

The defence force wearily took to their positions whilst some worked at building up the barricade blocking the east gate. Others carried jars of what oil and molasses remained to the parapet above the gatehouse. Able-bodied civilians, cooks and servants were issued with spears and told to form a last line of defence behind the soldiers. Guards at the north gate had stopped people from fleeing to the forest on the orders of Valorian. Men and women must all stand and fight.

The beat of war drums grew louder, and a blood-curdling cry went up from the Saxons who marched steadily on the east gate in a V-shaped formation, skirting around the walls of the abandoned amphitheatre. Cerdric rode behind a dozen men carrying a large tree, cut for use as a battering-ram, flanked by his guard, at the back of the marching 'V'. They were a formidable sight, with fewer numbers than the defenders, but all seasoned and ruthless warriors. Axes, swords and spears banged against shields, and the warriors chanted in unison as they advanced behind their shield wall. Quintus, Ahmed and

Drustan shouted words of defiance to try and rouse the spirits and quell the fears of their largely civilian defence force.

Polyamis, flanked by Camillus and Januarius, looked down on the approaching battering-ram from their position on the battlements above the east wall. "Look!" Polyamis cried, pointing to the pathway connecting the arena to the wall. "They are making for the side door!" A break-away group of twenty-or-so Saxons were rushing towards the door that serviced the abandoned amphitheatre.

"You should tell our commander," Camillus replied, "and I will spear one on my javelin."

Ahmed the Silent stood close by and Polyamis approached him and spoke hurriedly in Latin, "Commander, there are Saxons approaching a wooden door below us, an entrance to the amphitheatre. It is a door known to me and my friends, and we know there is but one wooden bolt holding it closed. Allow us to hasten there to brace it."

Ahmed eyed the keen ex-slave and paused to consider the possibility of betrayal before replying, "Go, with your companions, and two of my own," pointing to the wooden ladder.

Polyamis rushed back to his comrades and soon five men clambered down the ladder to the dusty earth and rushed to the vulnerable door. It was manned by a handful of worried citizens, who had rolled a cart into the stone doorway to partially block it. The five uniformed soldiers running towards them, carrying shields and spears, were a welcome sight.

"Hail fellows!" a trembling elderly man said. "We have been asking for soldiers, but to no avail."

Polyamis shouted to the group, "We have to strengthen the door now. Saxons approach!"

Just then, a deafening slam into the wooden door echoed in the arena, and the cart shook. In terror, the seven townsfolk threw the weight of their bodies against the cart, its rough timber digging into their backs and arms. Ahmed's man took charge of the locals and sent Polyamis, Januarius and Camillus to find something to brace the door. They soon returned, dragging a roof beam to the doorway. The cart was rolled away, and the beam was jammed against the stout oak door, as angry and determined warriors continued to batter it from the outside.

Volleys of arrows hailed down from the battlements onto the Saxons, who had broken into a charge, carrying their battering-ram straight at the barricade blocking the east gatehouse entrance. They rammed into the collection of wooden objects piled high by the gate, making it shudder.

"Get ready to pour oil!" Quintus shouted. "Flaming arrows to the ready!"

On the second charge with the battering-ram, the Britons tipped the remainder of the oil and molasses down onto the raised shields of the attackers. Flaming arrows were fired onto them, and the oil caught in a flash of orange heat that roared along the line of Saxons.

The men screamed in agony and tried to fling off the sticky molasses that bubbled and smoked as it fried on their skin; a demented, stomping dance in the flames ensued. Some victims stumbled blindly into the ditch, and others hurled themselves down in a desperate bid to escape their torment.

The survivors, undeterred, were joined by new men from the rear ranks who retrieved the ram and made ready for another assault. Fire now threatened the barricade within the gatehouse, and those nearest to it shouted for water to douse it. Cerdric was waving his good arm and urging his men on, sensing a breakthrough was imminent. Ahmed pulled his bow back and fired an arrow at him, which fell short, but near enough for Cerdric's guards to move him back a few paces.

The assault continued, and on their sixth ram into the barricade, Cerdric's warriors broke through. Quintus moved his soldiers back in a semi-circle away from the barricade and brought his archers to the front. As the wild Saxons squeezed their way through the pile of wood, they were easily picked off by the archers. Soon, the attackers had removed more wooden planks and were able to rush through in force, and bitter hand-to-hand fighting broke out.

Quintus, Ahmed and Drustan led by example, hacking and slashing at their bigger opponents. It seemed that two onto one was the only way to overpower these manic warriors, heavily protected by thick clothing, helmets and wooden shields. All knew it was a desperate fight to the end. It would be decided here, and women joined in beside their men, knowing that there would be no mercy shown should the Saxons prevail.

Two rows of housing along from the east gate, Polyamis's group were now fighting a hand-to-hand battle with a dozen determined Saxons who had forced their way through the side door. The five soldiers used their shields to parry blows from sword and axe and jabbed back with their spears, as they had been taught only days earlier. When the first two leaders of the townsfolk were slain, the others ran away, leaving the five plucky defenders to battle the marauding Saxons, who were high on blood lust.

"Back to the Mansio!" Polyamis yelled, as the they edged backwards in line until there was a wall behind them. The three friends, side by side, bravely fended off the assaults of their enemy, knowing in their hearts that Fortuna's blessing would soon end if reinforcements did not arrive. Pots and stools struck the heads of their bemused enemies, and Polyamis looked up to see Prisca and her fellow kitchen maids throwing missiles from the upper balcony of the inn. As if on cue, arrows rained down on the backs of the Saxons, from the battlements above, as their unit archers came to the rescue.

"Fortuna is with us!" cried Januarius, as he battled a much larger man.

Polyamis snatched a moment to look up and smile at his love. As he turned his head back to the fray, his vision was filled with the scarred face of a grimacing warrior who drove his sword into Polyamis's gut.

"Polyamis!" Prisca screamed from above.

Polyamis sank to his knees, his eyesight dimming and the noise of battle fading. A roar from Camillus was the last sound he heard as his enraged friend thrust his spear into the Saxon.

"The eagle, find the eagle..." he groaned, before he slumped forward to join the dead Saxon on the dusty earth.

ALONG THE ROMAN road called the Portway, horsemen appeared out of the western forest, trotting in two lines to the north of Calleva Atrebatum. A tired boy-sentry in the north tower raised a cry and soon word was sent to the east gate. The fifty-strong cavalry of retired soldiers, dressed in their Roman legionaries' uniforms and carrying long lances, rode past the town and turned in formation to face the battle raging around the east gate.

Marcus raised his sword and the riders trotted forward onto the meadow, following their standard bearer, and increased their pace to a canter. Finally, with a blood-curdling cry from their leader, they urged their steeds into a full gallop. Those fighting inside could hear the commotion outside and wondered what was happening. Guards on the walls waved and whooped enthusiastically, indicating to the hard-pressed defenders below that help was on its way.

The Roman cavalry charged, the sun glinting off their lance tips, and clattered into the Saxons milling around outside the gates. Amidst cries and oaths, they drew their swords and set about slashing on either side as the invaders fell back in disarray. Marcus fought his way to Cerdric, who sat on a big grey horse, flanked by his commanders and surrounded by his guards on foot. Slashing and stabbing to his left and right, Marcus, supported by two big Romans and his young companion, came face to face with the giant warlord.

Marcus could see his face was pale from loss of blood, and he could only move one arm in slow movements. As his supporters engaged the guards, he clashed swords with the enemy chief. The powerful arm of the Saxon warlord could still swing his axe, but Marcus could easily avoid its deadly blade. He ducked as the battle axe flashed over his head and spurred his horse forward, driving the point of his sword towards the big man's ribs. His leather jerkin offered little protection and the sharp blade drove into his flesh.

With a groan Cerdric toppled backwards off the horse, and Marcus swiftly dismounted to finish him off with practised thrusts of his gladius. He hacked at the thick neck of the dead man, decapitating him and removing the horned helmet. Marcus impaled the severed head on his lance and climbed back onto his horse. Holding the head aloft, plaited beard and flaxen hair dangling about the bloody shaft, he let out a primal, blood-curdling cry. Heads turned towards him, with dismay showing on the faces of Saxons. A mighty cheer went up from the east gate as the defenders drove the remaining Saxons out. Within a matter of minutes, it was over, as the surrounded remnants of the Saxon army were cut down. The blood-soaked victors cheered as Marcus rode through the gate, leading his troop of veteran soldiers, to be greeted as heroes.

Marcus dismounted and threw the head to a group of boys who shrieked with delight at their prize. They soon impaled it on a broken lance and ran around the square to the cheers of the relieved defenders. Marcus was embraced warmly by Valorian, who beamed as he said, "Hail Marcus! Saviour of Calleva Atrebatum!" The cry was taken up by the tired and relieved defenders. "Hail Marcus!"

"My lord," Marcus said, "may I present Lucius Macarius, formerly a centurion of the Fifth Legion, now leader of the retired soldiers' commune, some thirty miles to the west. They have willingly put on their uniforms one more time to come to our aid."

"And glad for one more tilt of our lances, my lord," Lucius added.

"You and your men are a welcome sight and will be our guests to celebrate this famous victory!" Valorian's relief reflected the mood of the townsfolk, who were aware that they had barely evaded a brutal slaying at the hands of fearsome invaders. Details organised ox-carts for the removal and burial of the bodies of the slain in pits beyond the town, and preparations were made for a feast.

Valorian took Marcus to one side. "My friend, these events have shown our need for a strong defence force. This must be your charge. We had come to depend on Rome for all, but now find ourselves beyond the cover of their broad cloak, at the mercy of barbarians from the wild fringes of the world."

Marcus relaxed his tense shoulders and looked at the town around him. "My lord, they have left us something to build on, a basis for our own society, bringing together the best of two worlds. But how can we stop this flow of invaders who come to take from us? We lack the numbers and are at the mercy of the whims of the Gods."

Valorian guided him away from the melee and up onto the battlements. "My dear Marcus, we are indeed in need of outside help. I can tell you now, in confidence, that our Christian priest has received word that the Bishop of Londinium, Guithelin, has travelled to plead with the young king of Armorica, Aldrien, to send troops to our aid."

"Why would he do so?" Marcus asked.

"Because they are our tribal cousins across the water. Many of our people have already fled there for sanctuary, since the first ravages of barbarians on our shores after the Roman interest in our welfare started to wane. The signs were there for many years for those who could read them. King Aldrien might see the benefits for trade and mutual cooperation in these uncertain times."

Marcus looked to the setting sun in the west, and the gathering of crows and ravens over the battlefield. "We can only hope," he muttered. "Hope and pray."

Chapter Nine

A FEELING OF quiet determination fell on Calleva Atrebatum in the days following the battle, as Saxon slaves were put to work repairing the damage to its walls and surroundings. Chief Valorian established his court in the upper floor rooms of the Forum at the town's centre and appointed new civic leaders and a magistrate to oversee the running of his tribal lands. He was less pleased to hear of the escape of his troublesome brother, Vortigern.

Marcus was relieved to be reunited with his mother, Morcant, his wife, Cordelia, and daughter, Esther. He was even more pleased to be presented with his baby son, Uther, who had been born at his father-in-law's farmstead. They made a home in the garrison commander's villa, where Marcus set about consolidating his defence force, ably assisted by Drustan, Quintus and Ahmed. He managed to keep one hundred men-at-arms, based in the barracks, but the remaining defenders opted to revert to their occupations in the town and surrounding farms.

GENTLE RHYTHMIC SNORING and the buzzing of flies were the only sounds in the barrack block as two soldiers slipped silently into the night. A pale moon lit their way to the outer walls, and they skirted the parade ground, making for the low wall surrounding the commander's villa. Marcus had no guard dogs, but they still froze in their tracks at the sound of growling and barking. This, they realised, was outside the barracks walls, and the noise of the roving pack soon diminished as it chased rivals through the cobbled streets.

The bigger of the two men led the way, hugging the walls around the courtyard, past the sounds of slumber from within bed chambers. The playful splashing of a fountain guided them towards the kitchen, and soon they were inside, blinking to accustom their eyes to the darkness and then opening a shutter where it would not be noticed to admit a shaft of moonlight. They searched for a cupboard with a trap door. Camillus and Januarius removed crates and sacks of vegetables and lifted the trap door to the secret cellar under the villa. They dropped down onto the soft clay and crawled in the darkness until they found a reed mat. After rolling it back, they scooped up the soil with pieces of a broken pot that lay about them, and soon unearthed the treasures hidden beneath.

Camillus unwrapped a cumbersome, heavy object and ran his fingers around the beak and head of the bronze eagle and along its cold outstretched wings. This was the prize that had inspired his friend Polyamis and would now buy them new lives in another place. Januarius clutched a bag of coins and jewellery as they made their way undetected back to the barracks and to the room where the kitchen maids slept. Prisca was waiting to receive the objects and hide them. Without words, she hugged the two soldiers, who returned quietly to their barrack bunks.

She sat on her straw-stuffed mattress admiring the intricate workmanship of the eagle in the weak light cast by a flickering candle. A smile stayed her grief as she thought of the audacity of her lover, Polyamis, in stealing such a powerful symbol of imperial Rome from his master. This bronze cast had inspired him to seek freedom not just for himself but for their band of runaways. He had chosen to fight as a free man, but his death had crushed her hopes for a new life together. Yet, by his actions he had secured her freedom and those of the other survivors – Camillus, Januarius and her two female companions. She offered a silent prayer for him to Fortuna as the pale fingers of dawn reached out across the wall. Wrapping her prizes in a cloak, she hid them under her cot and made ready for the new day.

PART THREE: CONSTANTINE

Chapter One

SEASICK SOLDIERS VOMITED over the sides onto the white caps of rolling green waves as the oarsmen below them pulled hard to avoid jagged rocks.

"Hard to the right!" a lookout yelled along the fifty-yard length of the wooden deck to the helmsman at the rear. Prince Constantine wrapped his red cloak tightly about him and glanced over the side at angry waves breaking on a jagged reef below towering white cliffs. Beside him stood the ship's elderly captain; his muscular ex-legionary deputy commander, Allectus; and the tiny Bishop Guithelin.

"This is the Isle of Vectis - a dangerous place for seafarers," the captain shouted into the wind. "We go around it to find the Roman port of Noviomagus on the south coast."

Constantine nodded, his brown curls wet with sea spray. "Do your job, Captain, and land us safely," he said, gripping the rope that would guide his way to his quarters below deck.

The lurching vessel sent the diminutive bishop bouncing off the cabin doorframe into his more robust companion, Father Damian, who gripped his master's arm to steady him. "Pray sit at the table, Master, until we find calmer waters."

Constantine sat huddled with his officers and attendants at a separate table from the Briton priest and bishop. Guithelin wondered if he already regretted agreeing to his brother's proposal to lead an army to Britannia and seize the blighted island for himself. As if reading his mind, Constantine called across to Guithelin.

"My Lord Bishop, are these stormy seas around your island a portent of doom for our enterprise, I wonder?" He was a moody warrior of twenty-two years who had supported his older brother, Aldrien, the King of Armorica and Benoic, as commander of his army. They had jointly agreed that he could be spared for his venture across the Gaulish Sea, since the borders of their lands now were guarded by a ring of well-manned fortresses. To the south, their allies the Romans kept four legions in the field to battle the Franks and Visigoths who had crossed the Rhine River and troubled the eastern lands. Aldrien was confident that their immediate threat was minimal.

"God smiles on your coming, my lord," Guithelin replied. "These seas are often stormy and help keep pirates and raiders at bay."

After some minutes of gut-clutching, quiet reflection, the door opened and the captain summoned them to the deck.

"We approach the harbour, my lord," he said, pointing to the stone headland turrets on either side whose metal grates were devoid of firewood and above which lone poles stood naked of flags. The fleet of ten ships slipped silently between them into a wide natural harbour whose calm waters reflected the blue sky.

"Saxon ships on the shore!" a lookout called, pointing ahead. They looked across the still water to a dozen boats beached on the shingle close by a row of deserted wooden piers.

"They are unguarded, my lord," an officer shouted, "and have been burnt."

THE FLEET GLIDED across the quiet millpond, tension on the faces of the men who readied themselves for an ambush. Gulls squawked above them as they drew close to the wooden piers, and the story of a port sacked and burnt by seaborne raiders came to the minds of the silent soldiers and crew.

"This did not happen in recent days," Allectus intoned in his deep voice. "There is no smoke from the ruins and the dead have been removed." They tied up the lead boats to the pier and jumped out to begin the search of the deserted and ruined port for clues as to what had happened.

"If only dogs could speak," Constantine said, pointing to timid curs skulking in the shadows of burnt warehouses. Just then a boy appeared from behind the rubble. Guithelin instinctively stepped ahead of the soldiers and turned to Constantine.

"My Lord, may I speak to the boy?"

"Go ahead. Find out what you can."

Guithelin and Damian cautiously approached the timid boy, who edged backwards.

"Do not be afraid," Guithelin said in the local dialect, holding his cross before him. "We shall not harm you."

Damian held out a crust of bread, and the boy stayed his ground until they reached him. The filthy barefoot boy, barely eight years of age, devoured the crust and then drank from the Priest's gourd.

"Tell us what has happened here, boy," Damian said.

He wiped his nose with the back of his hand and looked up at the young Priest, whose age must have been close to that of his father. "My lords, the Saxons came here some days ago and laid waste with terrible slaughter. They spared no one," he sniffed, his eyes welling up with tears.

Damian put a hand on his shoulder. "I can see you are a brave boy who has witnessed terrible things that no boy should see. Did you find a place to hide when they came?"

He nodded and pointed to a small hillock. "I was tending to the sheep. When the screaming started, I ran to a cave yonder and hid."

"And when you came out, what did you find?" Guithelin asked.

"I waited until nightfall and then watched the town burn. They were laughing, and the screams died away after a while. I walked to the next village and told them what had happened."

"Are there men who came to bury the dead?" Damian asked.

"Aye, my lord. They came and buried my family and my neighbours." He sobbed at the painful memory.

"Where are the Saxons now? Why have they not returned to their boats?"

The boy shrugged his shoulders and thought for a moment. "The men from the next village did fight the Saxons who had remained to guard their boats, killing them, Sirs. The ones from the boats did march up the road to Calleva but have not returned."

The priests exchanged looks and stood. Guithelin signalled to Constantine to come forward and then turned to the boy. "Will you lead this fine lord and his soldiers to the men from the next village, so we may question them?"

The boy looked doubtful. Damian crouched to eye level with the lad and said, "These are goodly folk who have come to protect our people from raiders. I promise you, they mean no harm to you or your neighbours. Come, you shall ride on my horse and I shall find some clothes for you to wear. What is your name, boy?"

"I am David, named by a Christian priest like you, sir."

"Then come with us David, so we may understand what happened here in Noviomagus."

SHIPS BERTHED TWO at a time on the one serviceable pier, spilling their loads of men, equipment and horses. Constantine conversed with his commanders and they decided to look for a suitable site for their camp, choosing the grounds of a burnt-down villa, whilst their Briton-speaking scouts scoured the countryside looking for hostiles or friendly locals.

"Allectus, you shall lead a dozen riders and go with the Priest and the boy to find the Regnii chief. Tell him we have come to aid the Britons in their fight against barbarian raiders - and ask about the fate of the Saxon war party." Allectus saluted his master and left the group to make his preparations. Constantine turned his attentions to offloading supplies and establishing a camp and invited Bishop Guithelin to eat with him in his tent.

Guithelin sat quietly at a table as liveried servants buzzed about him. He watched Constantine give out orders, getting the measure of the man who would be King of the Britons, whose close-set black eyes moved hungrily over a parchment map, looking down a hooked nose that gave the Prince the appearance of a rapacious hawk. Jerky movements of the curly head only added to the image. Before long Constantine joined him at the table and called for food and drink.

"What welcome do you expect from the chief of the Regnii?" he asked, filling his platter with Gallic delicacies.

Guithelin cleared his throat and replied, "My lord, I feel they may regard you with suspicion at first. You must win over this Regnii chief and persuade him to accompany you on your progress to Calleva. That town was the administrative centre for this area." He popped a sweetmeat ball into his mouth and sat back, chewing.

Constantine drank from a silver goblet and regarded the small man opposite him with his beady, unemotional eyes. "You are right, dear Bishop. These people have suffered at the hands of invaders and may regard us as no better. I shall make a gift to him and persuade him that we hold the same high standards of order and civility as the departed Romans."

"And yet, the chief will also want assurances of his rights and freedom to rule over his people, lord," Guithelin said. "They have come out from under the yoke of Roman rule and will be wary of a new master who could abuse them and tax them. I believe the smoothest path is to leave them free to follow their tribal ways, although they should be guided away from pagan gods towards the rightful worship of Christ our Lord."

Constantine blinked in annoyance and chased away a serving boy who had spilled some wine. "Yes, yes, of course. But that is too much for our first contact. I would want to gain their trust and backing first, as a military leader who can make safe this island. There will be a time to talk of God and faith, dear Bishop."

The two men lapsed into silence as attendants refreshed their goblets with a fine wine, one picking, the other pecking at dried fruits from a silver platter.

DAVID GUIDED THE line of riders off the coastal path and up a narrow ravine, climbing towards a patch of blue sky between high cliffs. A fresh sea breeze carried the smell of seaweed to their nostrils and put the taste of salt in their mouths as they picked their way between hardy sage brush, keeping the sea cliffs to their right.

"How much further, boy?" Allectus growled in a fractured, gravelly voice. He turned to look at David, sitting behind Damian and tightly clutching the Priest's quilted jacket, and in doing so dislodged the scarf that covered his throat, exposing a cruel jagged scar across his neck.

"Not far, My Lord," David replied, recoiling slightly at the sight of the battle scar. "We shall soon see a wooden fort through yonder trees."

Allectus had noticed them staring at his scar and said, "There are not many men who have survived having their throat cut, Father. I was slow in avoiding the swinging blade of a Frankish warrior. But he is now dead, and I am upright in the saddle." A grim smile played across his cracked lips, strands of his light brown hair playing about his weathered face.

"Your warrior life is writ large on you, Allectus," Damian cautiously replied. "Our Lord God has a purpose for you yet in our mission to bring security to this troubled land - for there will be need for men of courage, strength and dread resolve before we prevail."

"I fear it may not just be barbarian raiders we shall end up fighting," he replied, pulling his reins and leading them towards a screen of trees.

They picked their way in single file through a wooded copse carpeted with bluebells. Birds chirped a warning and David noticed a rabbit scurry under a bush. A scout returned to report a palisade of sharpened poles ahead. Allectus left his men under cover of the trees and slowly advanced with the Priest and boy onto the meadow that gave no cover from any arrows that might be fired from the fortress walls. He halted half way to the fortress and called Damian forward.

"The three of us shall approach the gates and talk to them," he growled.

"We have no banner and must hope they do not take us for Saxons," Damian replied.

"Put the boy in front of you in the saddle and lead on," Allectus said, pointing to the gates.

They approached slowly with outstretched arms and palms turned up, noting the fifty-or-so conical helmets and glinting spear tips that lined the battlements. The palisade clearly housed a village that stood between it and a sheer cliff of grey rock, rising two hundred feet, with a lookout post balanced on top.

"Stand your ground and state your business!" a guard shouted from the parapet above the gatehouse. Two flags fluttered on either side of him, one depicting a white hare, and the other a black boar.

"I am Allectus, commander of the army of Prince Constantine of Armorica. We come in peace to talk to your chief. We are guided here from the port of Noviomagus by your boy, David."

After a moment's silence they were told to wait whilst the chief was informed. Their horses chewed grass as they sat in the open, beyond a dry ditch, marvelling at the curved-shaped wall of sharpened logs, which enclosed the village of the Regnii tribe against the high cliff that protected their rear. The cawing of crows away to their left drew their attention to three decomposing bodies tied to cross-poles.

"Criminals or enemies?" Allectus wondered aloud, patting his horse's neck.

Damian crossed himself and replied, "I shall pray for our safe deliverance."

THE GATES OPENED, and a chariot drawn by two white horses led a dozen riders, in slow procession, across the bridge over the ditch and onto the meadow. A youth not much older than David held the reins of the fitful horses, curbing their desire to run free. Behind him stood a woman of proud bearing, with flowing hair the colour of a burning sunset contained in a gem-studded leather headband. She wore a silver fox fur around her shoulders over a blood red cloak. As she approached, Damian noticed the delicate blue swirls painted on her cheeks and a torque of silver around her neck.

She regarded the two men and boy and chose to speak to Allectus. "Hail travellers from across the Gaulish Sea. I am Queen Nathair of the Regnii. For what purpose have you come to my lands?"

Allectus bowed. "Hail Queen Nathair of the Regnii. I am Allectus. I command the army of Prince Constantine, brother of King Aldrien of Armorica. We come in peace and offer friendship to the tribes of Britannia."

"This is no longer Roman Britannia," she replied, raising her voice so her followers could hear. "This is the island of Albion, an ancient land of warrior tribes who are guided by the gods of the earth, water and sky, and of the animals that live in our forests. We are not looking for new masters."

Her followers cheered and whooped, raising spears and banging their cowhide shields.

Allectus glanced at Damian, who nodded and spoke to the queen, "My lady, I am Father Damian, a Christian priest from this land. It is Bishop Guithelin from Londinium who has sought the help of our friends in Armorica, who often have given refuge to Britons in flight from barbarian raids. They have come to the aid of our desperate fellows, who are beset on all sides by cruel invaders..."

"Thank you, Father," she said, cutting him short. "Let us discuss this matter further in my hall. How many men have you come with, Allectus?"

"Merely a guard of a dozen, my lady."

"Then summon them that they may also be refreshed." She tapped her driver on the shoulder and he expertly turned his team, making for the gatehouse. Allectus waved his men forwards and then led them through the gatehouse into a wide area lined with roundhouses and livestock pens. They followed the queen's procession along a compacted earth avenue lined with white stones to the rear of the compound, where stone steps chiselled from the rock led to a hall of stone carved into the cliff. Dull and dusty villagers gawped in silence as they passed.

Damian studied the home of their host as she ordered her dutiful attendants to bring chairs, food and drink. The hall was lit with oil lamps, and a fire roared in a large grate whose chimney funnelled the smoke to the outside. Hunting hounds lolled on bearskin rugs, paying little heed to the visitors.

"Please remove your cloaks and be at ease," Nathair purred, comfortable in her hall. She noted the tall, powerful frame of Allectus, and his many scars, as he sat. He noted the embroidered tapestry on the wall behind her throne, depicting two patterned snakes interwoven against a dark forest, their black eyes hungrily regarding all visitors, their forked tongues flicking a warning.

"You have seen many battles, Allectus of Armorica."

"Indeed, my lady. I have been patrolling the borders of our kingdom and fighting the Franks and Visigoths, who have crossed the wide river that once marked the boundary of the Roman world and now trouble our lands. To our south is the last

Roman army in the west. They are our allies as we look to keep the barbarians at bay."

"Many of our brave warriors left with the Romans when they departed. They were used to earning Roman coin in their auxiliary units. This has weakened us in our efforts to chase raiders from our coast."

Damian picked up this thread. "It is for this reason that we have come, my lady. The Armoricans are our natural brothers and share common enemies. They have taken in many Briton families, some of whose sons now return with Prince Constantine who offers his protection to our people."

She regarded them without expression whilst picking cured meat from a platter. "And how many men has Prince Constantine brought?"

Allectus replied, "My lady, he has come with a force of two thousand. King Aldrien could spare half that from his army, the remainder being Briton, Gaul and Roman volunteers."

"That is not a very big army," she said, eliciting the laughs of her courtiers.

"Indeed not, my lady," Allectus replied. "It is no invasion force. That is not my master's intention." After a pause he added, "My lady, we found the wreckage of many Saxon ships on the shores in the harbour and an abandoned port. Pray tell us, what misfortune befell that place?"

Queen Nathair briefly consulted an attendant and then fixed her hazel eyes on Allectus.

"We are used to raiders from Gaul, but the army that landed two moons past came in six dragon-headed longboats, as many as three hundred warriors, maybe more, thirsting for plunder. They descended on our people who lived in the old Roman port and killed them all. Some fled and came here to tell us."

Damian shook his head and tutted. Nathair ordered their goblets be replenished and continued.

"I led our warriors and we slew those Saxons who remained to guard their boats, recovering the stolen objects and children they had taken as slaves. I had no use for their boats and wanted to deny their fellows the chance to escape, so their ships were burnt. The main force had marched along the road towards Calleva. I sent scouts after them to report on their progress and we brought our dead here for burial."

"And did they return?" Allectus asked, leaning towards the young warrior queen.

"They did not. Our neighbours, the Atrebates, defended their town against the yellow-haired warriors from over the seas. These Saxons." She hissed the word. "There was a bloody battle around the town walls. Many of our warriors were trained in the Roman cavalry unit stationed there; they did fight well and vanquished the enemy. This is why the raiders never returned to their ships."

Allectus and Damian exchanged looks of surprise.

"This is a tale of noble deeds, my lady," Allectus said after a moment's reflection. "But why was there a Roman cavalry unit still there after the legions departed?"

"They were a unit of Britons led by half-Roman Marcus Aquillius, who remained - I know not how or why. But our scouts say they organised the townsfolk to fight."

Damian cleared his throat and spoke, "Are you friends with the Atrebates?"

Nathair glanced at her shaman, Brock, who laughed. "They are our cousins, but more powerful and numerous than us, and favoured by the Romans. Let me say that we pay homage to their chief, Tincomarus. Their town grew fat on Roman trade, and many legions passed through there on their way inland. Many of our young men and their women have left here to prosper in Calleva."

Over food and drink Allectus casually asked her, "And how was your relationship with the Romans?"

She glared at the mention of Romans. "We were treated as people who have been conquered – they took our finest young men and women, and insisted we quarry stones for them from the mountain at our backs. In exchange they gave us grain, salt and a few baubles…"

"…And some silver and gold for your husband," Brock whispered, his tattooed face cracking into a grin that revealed the sharpened points of his teeth.

"My late husband," she replied, silencing him with a cold stare.

Allectus broke the awkward silence that followed by standing as if to leave.

"Queen Nathair, I thank you for your welcome and hospitality. I would invite you to ride with me to the port and meet with Prince Constantine. He will be pleased to hear of this victory over Saxon raiders and would ask you to travel with us to

Calleva. It is there we shall talk to Tincomarus of the Atrebates about how we can help make your lands safe from raiders."

The queen leaned to her right and discussed the proposition with her advisers. Then she stood, flattened down her woollen skirt and approached Allectus. She looked up into the tall soldier's wide-set eyes and said, "It shall be so. We shall leave immediately and meet with your master before the sun dips to the west. The fate of our tribe, along with our neighbours the Belgae, is bound up in the decisions of Tincomarus and the Atrebates clan. Your coming was foreseen by my shaman, but we shall see if the portents are good."

Chapter Two

NATHAIR RODE BESIDE Allectus on a grey mare, its swishing, tangled mane and tail a match for the tumbling waves of her copper hair.

"Does your name have a meaning in your tribe?" Allectus asked.

"I was born just before the Beltane festival that banishes winter and welcomes the spring. My father named me after the dancing hares in the meadow." She laughed lightly, and he held her look, returning her smile.

"The hare is swift and powerful, my lady. You have been well named."

Their slow procession descended to the coastal path and entered a camp bustling with activity - men swarmed about, some shouting orders and others locked in disputes over petty matters, whilst horses dragged logs and yoked slaves carried pails of water. They all stopped to gaze in awe at the striking Queen, her red robe flowing behind her as she rode into camp, and Guithelin stepped forward to raise his neat bishop's hand in a blessing. Constantine shielded his eyes from the setting sun as he watched her dismount from the mare before handing her reins to a servant.

"Welcome lady," he said with a slight bow as she approached him, a few paces ahead of two of her own armed guards, her fingertips resting lightly on the arm of gallant Allectus. She stood between Constantine and the dying rays of the sun in an orange halo.

"May I introduce Queen Nathair of the Regnii, my lord," Allectus said, stepping to one side. "My lady, this is Prince Constantine, my general."

Constantine kissed her hand and drank in her wild beauty. She wore a silver torque around her snow-white neck, one end a snake's head, the other its tail. He met her level, green-eyed gaze and responded in kind to her warm smile, his enchantment complete.

"You honour us, Queen Nathair of the Regnii. I bring greetings from King Aldrien of Armorica and Benoica, my brother across the Gaulish Sea. I come in peace and wish to offer my aid to your cause against foul and savage invaders who trouble your land. Please, come to my tent for refreshment."

Allectus was curtly dismissed to see to preparations for the morning and was swallowed up by a forest of supply wagons and tents, joining the officers to whom the soldiers looked for orders that would see them and their mounts on the road, rested and with full bellies, on the morrow. Constantine was displeased with his deputy, who had not sent a scout ahead to brief him, and showed it in his petulant manner. He did not like surprises and the appearance of Nathair was certainly that, when he had expected the leader of the Regnii to be a gruff war dog.

The taste of roast fowl soon recovered his temper and Gallic hospitality won Nathair's co-operation. Sheltered from the sea breeze in Constantine's tent and warming good brandy wine in the cup of her hand, the Queen listened and nodded before airily agreeing to escort him to Calleva and commend him to her tribal overlord, Tincomarus of the Atrebates.

"But, my lord," she purred, setting down her silver goblet, "it is a two-day march for your foot soldiers, although riders can make it in one day. I propose we camp at the site of an inn that is half way along the road? My scouts also tell me that a bridge over a fast-flowing stream is in need of repair before horse-drawn carts may pass."

"I am your guest, my lady, and will follow your advice," Constantine crooned. "My men are still repairing carts we have salvaged and can follow us after two days, by which time my engineers will have repaired this bridge. Let us retire and break camp at dawn."

Nathair stood and smoothed down her woollen skirt, bejewelled armbands jangling. "I am heartily fed, and I thank you, Prince Constantine. I shall retire to my tent and be ready at first light." She left swiftly before he could extend his invitation and followed her guards, who led her by torch light to their camp. Allectus was waiting for her there.

"My lady, I have supervised the erection of your tent and wish you a good night." He bowed to her and kissed her hand.

"You are a thoughtful soldier, dear Allectus," she purred, rewarding him with a warm smile, touching him lightly on the arm. "I feel much safer in your company. Now I must bid you good night."

The tent flap fell behind her, leaving Allectus standing in the gloom. He slowly followed the line of burning torches to his own quarters, reflecting on a strange and magical day.

A LOW SEA mist hung over the soldiers the next morning, dampening their spirits as they broke camp. Constantine gave his orders to Allectus to remain behind with half of the men and follow once the carts were repaired and loaded with their equipment. He set off on the road to Calleva in the company of Nathair, leading two ranks of mounted soldiers followed by marching foot soldiers.

"Our way should be clear," she said as the hooves of their horses struck up a steady rhythm on the cobbled stones. Constantine rode beside her at the head of the army, admiring the change in scenery as the road climbed above the line of the cliffs and entered a forest.

"You are my guide in this wild place," he quipped, patting the neck of his snorting black stallion that stood a hand taller than her spirited grey mare. Unseen creatures scurried in the undergrowth.

"I have sent my scouts ahead to check on the place where we shall camp and the bridge just beyond," she said.

"My engineers are with us," Constantine replied, "and can make planks of wood from these fine trees. Perhaps we shall hunt wild boar for our supper?"

She laughed and smiled at her royal guest. "Yes, my lord, we shall hunt boar in the forest – there are many."

By mid-afternoon they had covered over twenty miles to the clearing cut from the forest where the ruins of a stone building lay surrounded by burnt beams and spars. Animal pens and outhouses had also been ransacked and there was no sign of life, except for a pack of feral dogs slinking away into the dark forest at the sound of their approach.

"This was the Halfway Inn, run by my cousin's family. They were slaughtered here by Saxon scouts who came before their army." She pointed to a row of graves that had been dug up, leaving bones and rags of clothing exposed about the burial site.

"My scouts found the dead and buried them here, but it seems the animals have also found them."

They dismounted, and Constantine barked some orders to his men to repair the graves.

"The spirits of the unhappy dead hang over this place, perhaps prevented from passing to the Otherworld until they are avenged," Nathair remarked, kicking lumps of scorched wood.

"We Christians believe that the just go to Heaven and the unjust go to Hell," Constantine replied.

"Your 'Hell' is the same place as the Romans' 'Hades', no doubt," her shaman, Brock, commented, grinning at Father Damian through sharpened fangs. "Your feast days are also borrowed from the Romans, and now you take their temples and call them churches."

Father Damian would not be goaded and smiled benevolently at his dirty companion. "God was always guiding the Romans towards the light of His truth. It is not surprising that these changes have been made as people turn away from pagan worship and embrace the One True God."

Constantine made an unpleasant squawk by way of laughter. "You would be advised not to argue with a priest – they have an answer to every question!" He twitched as he preened his dark hair. Nathair glared at her impudent shaman and took her leave, followed by her guards to a corner of the clearing where they set up camp. Soon fires were burning, and tents had sprung up around the clearing as men set about the tasks of fetching water and preparing the evening meal.

Two days later, Allectus joined them with the horse-drawn wagons and remaining foot soldiers. Constantine's engineers had found two tree trunks crudely positioned across the span of a collapsed bridge and set about restoring it to a sturdier construct. The repairs were completed in two days, and the entire army with wagons were able to pass over the narrow gorge above the dancing white caps of a fast-flowing river. The army of two thousand advanced through a narrow passage between two cliffs, noting splintered rocks dropped from above and the remains of shattered shields and spears. Their progress was undisturbed as the road climbed gently towards the plateau on which a once-Roman garrison town sat.

THE SOUNDS OF an excited crowd running along the lane beyond his villa wall had become a distraction for Marcus. He looked up from his parchment map of Britannia Prima at the sound of horns blowing from the gatehouse and of hobnail boots echoing along the corridor.

"Sir, I have ridden hard this last hour. An army approaches Calleva from the south," Marcus's dusty scout puffed.

"Is it a friendly or hostile approach?" Marcus demanded.

"They come in peace, led by Queen Nathair and her Regnii warriors."

Marcus exchanged a glance with his deputy, Drustan, and they both instinctively buckled their sword belts and reached for their Roman helmets as they headed for the door.

"Call out the guard!" Marcus yelled as he stepped into the courtyard, the pale spring sunshine barely casting shadows as they strode purposefully towards the gate that separated the commanding officer's quarters from the barracks. "March the men to the south gatehouse, then have them fall-in on either side to form a guard of honour. I'll go to the Forum to seek out Chief Valorian."

Drustan saluted and hurried off.

Barely a month had passed since the desperate defence of their town, and now repairs had been made to damaged walls and the dead buried in burial mounds on the edge of the clearing, dug by a work party of thirty or more Saxon slaves. Marcus made his way past chattering townsfolk and yapping dogs, past cattle and horse pens and two-storey terraced townhouses on his way to the high four-sided building that dominated the centre of the town - the Forum.

"...and the store room was left unlocked for any pilferer to make free with my goods. Why do we not simply invite the Saxons to return!" Valorian paced across the marble floor of what was once the regional governor's reception room, the impassive stares from Roman Gods and titans looking through him. He appeared to be railing at unresponsive servants.

Marcus fidgeted patiently until Valorian turned and noticed him.

"Ah, Marcus, your arrival is timely. Our cousin Nathair, of the Regnii, approaches our gate with a force of soldiers who have come from Armorica, across the sea. We shall greet them in peace and uncover their intentions."

Marcus, not yet twenty years, had grown in confidence and stature since he had stood firm in the face of Cerdric's fearsome Saxon invaders, commanding a defence force numbering over three hundred that included army veterans and men twice his age. Now he remained with a standing garrison of one hundred and fifty men, the others released to return to their farms and trades.

"I have sent the men to the south gatehouse to form a guard of honour, m lord."

"Excellent. Now we shall await them here, in the magistrate's chamber. Instruct your deputy to bring them to us and ensure the remaining barrack blocks and stables are prepared."

Constantine was impressed by the carefully maintained clearing that the road spilled onto, on a wide and flat plateau dominated by a walled town in its centre. To the right of the town walls stood an enclosed amphitheatre, connected to the town wall by a footpath lined with statues of long-gone Emperors and assorted Roman gods. He followed the line of Nathair's look to a row of freshly dug burial mounds to the far right of the clearing, just before the line of trees, then his gaze fell on the ruin of a camp and the evidence of conflict.

"The land tells its own story," he remarked flatly.

She turned to him and replied, "Not only Saxons are buried there but many of our own. There was great bloodshed here on this plain after a full day of fighting."

"Then the war has come to Britannia. It is ever so in Gaul, where the once invincible Romans are chased across the land by wild tribesmen who can smell weakness and sense opportunity."

They moved at a lazy pace over a stone bridge spanning a dry ditch and through the wide gatehouse, passing from sunlight into shade and then out again, to a rapturous welcome by townsfolk throwing flower petals and hooting at the dusty riders and cheerful foot soldiers who followed. Constantine noted the familiar two-storey buildings, their balconies festooned with hanging washing and cheering families, and the soldiers in part-Roman uniforms lining the street, who looked straight ahead in a manner that spoke of discipline.

"This is indeed a Roman town," he remarked to his proud escort.

"They are the people of this place, since time began, and have outlasted their occupiers. They are happy now, but also wary after fighting off invaders," Nathair replied with a cheerful smile.

Three officers on horseback approached them and Constantine held up his arm to signal a halt.

Drustan shouted above the din of the crowd, "On behalf of Chief Valorian of the Atrebates, I welcome you to this town of Calleva Atrebatum. I am Drustan, deputy commander of the garrison, and am instructed to guide you to the Forum to meet my masters." With a bow, he turned his horse and led the visitors towards the centre of the town and the impressive building which dominated it.

VALORIAN RECEIVED HIS visitors in the splendour of the magistrate's hall, with shafts of sunlight from high windows illuminating tapestries of hunting scenes that adorned the opposing wall. He had been reading out a roll of honour when Constantine's dust cloud was spotted and was still in his finery, a robe of white linen lined with gold silk and the purple cloak of a Roman Governor. His long dark brown hair was contained by a filet of gold, and around his neck a silver torque with bulbous ends confirmed his high status.

The nobles greeted each other warmly whilst Marcus and Allectus sized each other up. Bishop Guithelin and Father Damian were welcomed by the local priest, Father Andreus. Guithelin appeared even smaller than usual, worn out after his unaccustomed journeying over land and sea, and kindly Father Andreas declared he would later boil nettles and prepare a tonic for him. The kitchen hands had put up trestles and were still setting out bowls and chargers for a hurriedly mustered banquet, but wine and ale flowed from the moment the thirsty travellers arrived.

Marcus noted the furtive looks exchanged between Nathair and Allectus as Valorian made a welcome toast and wondered what bonding had taken place on the journey from the south coast. Once food and drink had been consumed, the talk turned to the purpose of the visit.

"...and so, my noble brother, King Aldrien, passed the task to me to come to the aid of the tribes of Britannia, who will soon be facing an onslaught by the sea-borne invaders you have recently had a glimpse of. Their numbers seem infinite, as we have witnessed in eastern Gaul, and the Roman army has retreated westwards before them. Let us band together and see to the defence of this island."

Constantine's speech was greeted with thoughtful silence, and he hurriedly sat down as Valorian consulted his tribal elders before replying, "My lord Constantine, many of our sons and daughters departed with their Roman masters, and this latest report of their continued retreat affects us. Some nurse a hope for their return. However, already this island is returning to the tribal chiefdoms of the old times, and each chief jealously guards their lands. With caution, we welcome your timely offer of assistance, my lord, but know now, there is no vacant throne on this island."

All eyes fell on Constantine, whose black eyes blinked but who otherwise sat motionless. He reached for his goblet, composing his response. This came after a slow sip of wine and a dab at his black beard with an embroidered kerchief. "You are wise beyond your years, my lord Valorian," he said, rising to his feet, "and will no doubt have more appetite for this alliance when the boot of the invaders is on your throat. But by then it will be too late to organise a defence across tribal lands. I speak of raising a standing army that can meet your foes head on and crush them. Word will soon speed to their lairs, on the wings of crows, that Britannia is guarded and no place for easy plunder. You have already confronted the ferocity of these savages from beyond the Germanic Sea, and barely survived." He paused to take in the pensive faces of those around the table, knowing his words carried weight.

He drank some more in a nonchalant manner but remained on his feet. "Already those devils have a foothold in your eastern kingdom of Ceint. More will come unless you band together with your neighbours to drive them out. What you lack is military experience. This we have and can bring to your cause." He turned to Allectus and motioned him to stand.

"Here is Allectus – a veteran commander of many battles against the Franks and Goths, foul people whom the Romans failed to subdue, who have swept into our lands. This same fate awaits you unless you act now." Constantine at last sat down and waited for a response as Valorian and Marcus whispered to each other.

Valorian pushed back his chair and stood, pulling his gold-edged sleeve and clearing his throat. "Your speech carries a dark omen of misfortune, my lord. We might pray that this evil passes us by, but the evidence of recent events warns us also to defend ourselves, and stoutly. Without Roman legionaries we are thinly defended, and our tribal lands may be overrun one by one. However, we still have the benefit of their language and learning. I might suggest that my lord's cause would meet less resistance if he styled himself as 'Dux Bellorum', in the Roman fashion, rather than king. The dignity of our chiefs would thus be preserved."

He paused as quizzical looks and whispered questions were exchanged. "This is a landless lord who is a leader in battle, rallying the armies of several lords to a common cause. Dismiss, my lord, all suggestion that you would insist on fealty as the King of Britannia." He turned to the chief of the Regnii. "What say you, dear cousin Nathair?"

The brooding queen stood and pressed her palms on the table, her russet ringlets tumbling forward over her shoulders.

"My noble cousin, you would be wise to ask that question of your own father, Chief Tincomarus, whom I hear still lives."

Valorian smiled and swiftly replied, "My father is old and bedridden, and his mind has wandered to the Netherworld, where he awaits his passing. He has handed me the right of chieftainship - his steward, Malthus, can attest to this - and I now wear his royal cloak and bloodstone ring." He showed his ringed hand as the steward bowed his confirmation.

"And what of your brother, Vortigern?" she asked. "Does he share in his father's inheritance?"

Valorian glared at her and snapped, "My villainous brother led the Saxons to our gates, hoping they would clear his path to leadership of our tribe." He checked himself, realising that he had been goaded into losing his temper. "But that is a family matter I will discuss with you after this meeting. Just know that I am overlord of these and your lands."

She smiled sweetly and replied, "Your brother is not welcome in my lands, dear cousin, as we have suffered greatly at the hands of those Saxon devils."

"Quite so," Valorian said, swaying slightly and unsure what to say next, his train of thought broken.

Constantine grinned and pushed himself to his feet. "My thanks for your wise counsel, Chief Valorian. Your brief exchange with the queen of the Regnii affords me a vision of what to expect from your fellow tribal chiefs. They will be wary of my coming, therefore we must do what we can to put them at their ease. I accept your proposal to offer my services to your Council of Chiefs as their military leader. Now let me propose a toast to our new partnership, and the wish that many chiefs join our cause to keep this land free of invaders, so that all may enjoy your new-found freedom."

Guithelin turned to Father Damian and whispered, "The hard part will be convening a Council of Chiefs as they already eye each other with jealousy and ambition."

"God will show us the way through our prayers, Your Eminence, for He will not abandon his followers in their hour of need," Damian replied, his eyes shining at the prospect of a hitherto unlikely peace.

Chapter Three

THE EAST WING of the Forum buildings was given to Constantine and his officers by Valorian, who brushed aside all questions from his circle concerning the duration of their stay. As the weeks passed, messengers were dispatched to all chiefs in the three former Roman provinces that covered southern, central and western Britannia. The lands to the North, much troubled by Pict and Votadani raiders from beyond of The Wall, could wait for another time.

Allectus, ten years older than Marcus and with the scars to support his tales of battles, quickly became a useful tutor for the young commander. Marcus gave him a tour of the barracks and half of the barrack blocks were cleared out and given over to Constantine's men. Allectus chose to stay close to his Master in the Forum, but most days would join Marcus to discuss military matters and take part in joint training exercises.

"Too few chiefs have deigned to reply to Lord Valorian's invitation to a council," Allectus said, his broad face and narrow blue eyes regarding Marcus impassively across the map table.

Marcus stood and poured spring water into two pewter mugs and offered one to his burly companion. "Aye, Valorian has spoken to me of his worry that no one will come. He wants us to ride out and encourage the ones nearest to commit to attend."

"Would that be with a sizeable band of riders to persuade them that it would be in their interest to attend?"

Marcus was not so inclined to get drawn into antagonism with neighbouring chiefs but could see the benefits from closer ties. "They should come willingly, or any union would be weak. If they stay away and wait until they are attacked, then it may be too late for them..."

"Then they must be persuaded," Allectus said, standing abruptly as if making a challenge.

"There is no law in this land, now the Romans have gone. Valorian has no right to summon them, nor Constantine who is a foreign prince in this land. All we can do is argue the case for safety in an alliance. However, they will not want any interference in their own affairs."

"They will listen to you, Marcus. You must tell them of your experiences here and how you faced down a determined Saxon war party. You must make them believe that their time will come and when it does, they can call on assistance from us."

"Then we become a roving band of warriors who will engage with invaders wherever they may appear? That will be a full-time occupation," Marcus replied.

"That is our job, Marcus. We are the defenders of the lands abandoned by Rome. It is a noble occupation."

Marcus smiled. He longed to ask his companion about his unusual looks – his wide head, fair curly hair and blue, almond-shaped eyes. Where had he come from?

As if reading his mind, Allectus set down his mug and smiled. "You look at me with questions, my friend. Then let me tell you. My father was a Roman auxiliary cavalry commander, recruited from his village far to the east, beyond many rivers and over mountains. His people are the Alani – skilled horse warriors of wide flat lands I have heard of but never set eyes on, skilled with bow and lance. The Romans defeated them and then recruited the men for their legions. He came to Gaul and fought against the Goths, a despised enemy of his tribe. That was the way of the world – men would fight their neighbours, not for their people but for the honour of Rome."

He saw he held Marcus's attention and continued, "I am his son and have inherited his sword, bow and lance, following him into his unit at a young age and learning the skills of a mounted warrior. We can ride as we shoot from the bow, which you may yet witness on this island if we fight together. There are many soldiers from faraway places in the Roman army. And even here, I see you have men from Nubia and Egypt in your ranks. The Romans have scooped us up and scattered us across the Earth, but now we forge our own destiny and fight for our lord. That is the way of it."

Marcus nodded and replied, "my father was also from a distant land. He came here as an Optio in the Fifth Legion and was then promoted to Centurion. His bones are buried to the north, near the Great Wall of Hadrian, no doubt, where he was last posted. My only memory of him is of hugging his thick thigh when I was a babe, barely able to stand. My mother is a Briton of the local tribe to this place, the Atrebates. I have now taken her Briton family name, Pendragon, to cement my loyalty to my chief and to our tribal ways. We have much in common, Allectus of the Alani."

They walked out into the sunlight and made their way to the Forum. Marcus felt more at ease in the company of the previously unknown, brooding warrior by his side, although he knew they served different masters. After a brief discussion with their leaders, it was agreed that they would ride out in the morning with a mounted escort to visit the surrounding chiefs and gauge their reaction to the call to a council.

"...And urge them to set aside petty matters and make haste to Calleva Atrebatum, where our hospitality awaits them," Valorian shouted at the backs of the burly commanders.

THREE MONTHS OF travel cemented their friendship and they formed a good team, with Marcus applying gentle persuasion backed-up by the silent menace of Allectus and his horse warriors. Leaves were falling from the trees and the harvest festivals completed by the time a dozen tribal chiefs met with Valorian and Constantine at the Forum building in Calleva.

Constantine shifted with cowed unease in the company of so much brawn but knew he must act the part of a confident and wise leader. After listening to Valorian's eloquent proposal and the suspicious grunts and whispers from the assembled chiefs, he stood, his beady hawk's eyes flitting from one unsmiling face to another. Even Queen Nathair sat in stony silence.

"You have described me as 'foreigner', and yet we are brothers sharing similar languages and customs. Although the Gaulish Sea separates us, history has seen us all suffer defeat and humiliation at the hands of Rome's legions. They forced us to give up our sons to the cause of expanding Rome's empire. Over time, many of us bent to Roman ways - some ways better than others."

He paused to sip from his goblet, eying his attentive audience. "But now Rome has gone from your island and you are free. I will not change that. You are the leaders of your people and shall remain so. What I propose to you is a new alliance, with my brother, King Aldrien. He sends to you my services as a leader, for I am familiar with those barbarians attacking your island from the east. They are an enemy we have fought for many years. I offer to train and lead your army as its commander, and in return would sit on your council to represent my noble brother."

"But what of those chiefs who are not here – Mandubracius of the powerful Trinovantes and the other tribes to the east?" a gruff bearded chief asked.

Constantine smiled, sensing that they were at least considering his proposal. "We shall raise an army that shall march under all your banners and go to persuade those who are not yet with us to join our cause. I would then post garrisons at the many coastal forts on the east and south to repel all seaborne invaders."

"And what of the Scotti who raid our west coast and march inland, seizing our possessions and women?" one asked.

"Aye, and the devilish Picts who raid over Hadrian's Wall?" another added.

Constantine raised his hands to quiet the hall. "Yes, there is much to be done, and in time an army shall travel north to persuade the northern chiefs that their lands too could be protected. There is much work to be done in this abandoned outpost of the Roman World if you are to confront the task of securing your lands from those who would rape and pillage. And they will come."

Constantine was joined by Valorian who raised his goblet and asked for their consent. A chorus of 'Aye' rang out around the table, and the mood lightened further when servants brought platters of food and more jugs of ale.

THE SHRILL CRY of a partridge flushed from the undergrowth drew a giggle from Nathair and an instinctive glance around from Allectus.

"Our fellow hunters will soon come searching for us," she said, her hot breath on his face as she locked her arms around his thick neck. He bent towards her and their lips met, his wide-set almond eyes locking onto her beguiling green gaze. Her hands slipped to his bulging biceps, betraying her lust for this powerful man.

"Then we must make the most of these precious moments," he replied, his deep rumbling tone sending a shiver through her body, adding, "for this hunter has captured the hare."

She had waited patiently, feigning nonchalance at the suspicious glances of her cousin and the lustful advances of Prince Constantine. She had kept them both at arms-length, waiting for her opportunity to meet in secret with her warrior paramour.

Allectus picked her up by her slender waist and guided her to a patch of grass surrounded on three sides by a wall of dense holly that had colonised a cluster of rowan trees, their green and red berries jousting together for dominance. She willingly assented to his advance and pulled up her riding skirt to her thighs, encouraging him to drop his breeches and fall to his knees. With a groan he was upon her, and she responded with her own sighs, grabbing a handful of his thick woolly hair. She gazed up to a patch of blue sky framed by overhanging trees, which seemed to sway and nod their approval of her silent prayer to the gods of the forest that his seed be planted in her womb.

Chapter Four

WAR DRUMS ANNOUNCED the advance of the eastern Britons, who descended from their hilltop towards the line of men bunched on a meadow with their backs to a stream. The marching warriors with blue swirls painted on their cheeks and hair tied back in plaits roared their defiance and banged their oval shields with spears and sickles, the trampling hooves and wooden chariot wheels behind as perilous to them as the enemy in front.

At their rear Mandubracius looked on, flanked by his fellow chiefs and Vortigern, who was once again opposing his older brother, Valorian. "They have fewer men in the field below," he sneered, pointing with a sword. "We shall have little trouble slaying them and chasing this upstart Gaulish prince back to his country."

Vortigern was less sure, having witnessed the successful defence of Calleva from the perspective of the vanquished Saxon war party. "Their riders are nowhere to be seen, my lord. They will join the fray for sure from behind the hill."

"That may be so," Adomarus of the Cantii replied, "but we have our own mounted warriors and chariots in reserve. We shall swat them aside like flies."

On the opposing hilltop, Constantine, Allectus and Marcus surveyed the scene before them. Their small group of warriors had their orders to turn and jump across the stream and flee towards them just before their opponents reached their Roman shield wall. They had Briton cavalry and Allectus's mounted archers to introduce to the battle, and a healthy reserve of a thousand foot-soldiers waiting eagerly behind them to rush down the hill.

"Our cavalry will show themselves first," Constantine said, "as we planned, to draw out their riders. Allectus, go lead your army, my friend, and Marcus, time now to join your men. I shall lead the reserves in once they have fully committed." Marcus and Allectus bowed and rode in opposite directions to join their riders.

The two sides clashed with thunderous noise. Constantine's soldiers defended their side of the stream from their screaming foes, who waded across to charge head-on into their shields. His chariot riders were forced to deviate to the sides, riding along the stream until they found fording points.

"Sound the charge!" Constantine yelled, and six trumpets screeched another assault into the fray. Allectus and Marcus cantered their horsemen onto the field from opposing sides, engaging with the charioteers and riding towards the melee on the meadow. Allectus's mounted archers caused panic amongst the Britons who were unfamiliar with this deadly skill.

Mandubracius unleashed his mounted reserves, who swept down the hillside and splashed across the stream. "Ah ha, we have them now!" he yelled at his grim-faced entourage.

Cries and screams filled the valley as both armies slashed and hacked at each other. Allectus's archers made short work of the charioteers and unschooled riders, and Marcus led his heavily-armoured cavalry into the body of the opposing armies' foot-soldiers. Their numbers may have been evenly matched, but superior tactics and training made a telling difference in favour of Constantine's army. A second trumpet blast announced the arrival of two rows of foot-soldiers, led by Constantine on his prancing black stallion.

"They have more reserves!" Adomarus yelled, pointing his spear tip across the valley. Mandubracius stared in silent rage, realising he had been out-witted.

"We must join the battle with our escorts!" Gwethin yelled at his brother, pulling at Mandubracius's cloak.

"You lead them, brother, and may the gods of our ancestors guide your sword to the neck of that foreign prince," Mandubracius snarled.

Gwethin, snorting like a bull, seized his chance to join the battle, summoning their escort of thirty riders, together with Aldomarus and those Cantii nobles with the stomach for a fight. With a spleen-slicing scream, they swept down the hillside, leaving Mandubracius and scheming Vortigern to look on.

After barely an hour of fighting, Vortigern called for his horse. "The day is lost, my friend, and now I must venture north to seek further aid for our cause."

Mandubracius rounded on the younger man. "You have brought us to this field with your silver tongue, promising us victory over your brother and the Gauls. Now you run away like a scolded schoolboy. I have a mind to have your head!" He pulled his sword from his scabbard and swung it in a circle above him. Vortigern swiftly jumped into his saddle and galloped away with his two attendants, leaving the Trinovantes chief to gag on the bitterness of defeat.

"THE DAY IS WON!" Constantine declared as he rode between two ranks of cheering soldiers. They had not slaughtered all of their opponents as Marcus had pleaded with Aldomarus to surrender, once the outcome had become inevitable, promising no slaughter of captives or reprisals against rebellious tribes. As a fellow Briton, he was keen to sue for peace so there would not be bad blood between the tribes. Rows of dejected warriors hung their heads in shame as their hands were tied behind them.

"There will be no trophies taken. The slain shall be buried in pits as befits warriors of our island! Bring the prisoners to our camp beyond the hill, and their leaders shall meet with us there," Marcus shouted, taking the lead on the resolution to the brief but bloody battle. Mandubracius had fled, but they had his brother, Gwethin, and the chiefs of the Icenii and Cantii.

Constantine grinned his pleasure as he rode beside his champion, Allectus. "We have subdued this resistance and will gather more support as a result."

"Aye, my lord," Allectus replied, "you are wise to allow Marcus to take the lead, for we shall need the co-operation of the Britons if we are to succeed."

"He has passion and wisdom beyond his years," Constantine smugly noted. "You must keep him close, Allectus, for there is still much to be done."

WINTER FELL ON Calleva six months after the battle, with heavy snow before the Saturnalia festivities commenced. Vocal resistance had melted into a grudging cooperation from many chiefs, who sent small numbers of men to join a defence force based at Calleva. This pleased Constantine, as it weakened their ability to resist a centralised authority, but perturbed Valorian, who saw Calleva's population growing with little debate about the costs of keeping a standing army.

In the main hall of the Forum, Valorian held court, dealing with disputes between farmers and between neighbours in the town. Punishments were usually in fines, but there was also the threat of a public flogging or having a hand cut off for more serious offences - and death by hanging for the most serious. Constantine kept out of his way most of the time, and they had agreed to meet in the evenings to discuss matters of mutual interest over supper. Valorian had been formally accepted as Chief of the Atrebates following the death of his father a month earlier. He was also high chief over the lesser tribes of the Regnii and Belgae, who populated the lands to the south.

Constantine was keen to keep his small army under Allectus and Marcus in the field, cajoling chiefs into paying a tribute towards the costs of feeding and arming soldiers and building defences.

"Our army should sweep the south coast after the winter festivities to reassure the people of our intent to offer protection," Constantine remarked to Valorian.

"I am more concerned with the cost of housing them. We have not agreed any formal system of taxation with the chiefs, and the amounts they give grudgingly to Marcus and Allectus hardly pay for their salted herring and ale."

"But they are adjusting to the idea of a combined army to defend at least the southern half of the island," Constantine said, popping a grape into his mouth. "This is progress."

Valorian nodded in agreement. "After the winter storms have passed, perhaps. At least we have been spared any serious raids these past few months."

"But they will come on spring tides, and we must be ready for them. I propose that we send our men to assess the strength of the Roman forts along the coast and leave small garrisons there. There must be beacons ready to be lit and riders ready to carry the news of invasion."

"You are right," Valorian conceded. "But let us wait for the worst of the weather to pass."

IN THE TOWN there was much activity as both Christians and Pagans prepared to celebrate mid-winter's day in differing fashions. For the Christians it was the birthday of Christ, but older rituals were being prepared by the Pagans to mark the winter solstice. Bishop Guithelin, eager to return to his diocese in Londinium to mark the festival, instructed the town's priest, Father Andreus, in his duties.

"I plan to leave soon and return to my diocese, but before I go I wish to preach a sermon to your faithful. Christ's Mass presents an opportunity for you to win new souls to our faith." They walked along a straight, busy thoroughfare, past market stalls and cattle pens, northwards from the Forum towards the north gatehouse. The Christian church, a modest building of timber, dry mud walls and thatched roof, stood close by the north gate, away from the temples that clustered around the Forum.

"I shall preach the words of Saint Augustine to your faithful. He eloquently explained how the Church came upon the date of

Jesus the Christ's birth thus: 'Hence it is that He was born on the day which is the shortest in our earthly reckoning and from which subsequent days begin to increase in length. He, therefore, who bent low and lifted us up, chose the shortest day, yet the one whence light begins to increase'."

Andreus nodded to the diminutive bishop, who was no longer the worn traveller of their first meeting. "Your Eminence, it is a day also celebrated by our pagan neighbours, both from the Roman and Briton traditions, where they give offerings to their gods and also talk of the re-birth of the light..."

"Indeed," Guithelin agreed, "and it is no coincidence that the early Fathers of our Church took some inspiration from the pagan calendar, so that those who are drawn to our faith may continue to celebrate, though their voices be henceforth lifted to the one God. And now let me pray with our faithful and bid them farewell."

He entered the building and paused as his eyes adjusted to the gloom. High openings let in a little winter light and drafts of air that fed the flames of the oil lamps lining the wall, flickering shadows onto a bright painted frieze and animating its scenes from the Bible. After inhaling the comforting woody and woolly scents of incense and damp humanity, and then stifling a sneeze, Guethelin stepped lightly to the simple alter. There he turned to face the many Callevans, standing in rows before benches, who had gathered to wish him God-speed, acknowledging their respectful smiles and nods with his own modest bow.

Chapter Five

TRUMPET BLASTS ANNOUNCED the arrival of Constantine and his army at the west gate of Londinium. They had travelled at a leisurely pace from Calleva, following the Portway Road east, to Stanes, where they camped for one night before crossing the Ap Pontes Bridge over the River Tamesis. The following morning, they progressed the remaining seven miles to the west gate of Londinium, where they waited before closed gates.

Constantine had persuaded Bishop Guithelin to delay his return to his diocese until the flowers and early buds of Spring adorned the roadside meadows. "Ride ahead, dear Bishop, together with Marcus, and announce our arrival. Tell them we shall camp our army outside their walls and enter in peace to speak with their leaders." Their intelligence had suggested that Mandubracius had returned there to lick his wounds after his defeat in battle some six months earlier. The time had come for Constantine to force a further confrontation and to take possession of Britannia's largest and most influential town.

After an hour Marcus returned. "My lord, Bishop Guithelin is hailed a hero for his fruitful appeal to King Aldrien. The town Elders have invited you and your attendants to meet with them in the Senate. They inform us that Mandubracius and his followers fled in the night at news of your approach."

Constantine shared a smile with Allectus. "This is indeed good news. Allectus, tell the men to make camp. Then join us with a guard of twenty and we shall follow Marcus to meet with them."

They rode into empty streets, the faces of children staring curiously out from between balcony supports on the upper floors of townhouses until Guethelin was recognised. Then the Bishop's excited supporters crowded on either side of his horse shouting greetings, as he led the unknown prince and his guards to the centre of the town.

GUITHELIN WAS REUNITED with his committee of administrators and tax collectors, who now offered their services to Prince Constantine, should he take on the mantle of authority. The Trinovantes hierarchy had all fled to the nearby town of Camulodunum, taking whatever plunder they could muster. Constantine, encouraged by Guithelin to fill the vacuum, assumed command of the town. His endorsement by Bishop Guithelin was good enough for the inhabitants of this busy trading port who wanted little more than to continue their business with minimal interference.

Constantine moved his entourage into the Imperial buildings and surrounding villas, vacated by Mandubracius and his followers, and garrisoned his army in the Roman fort that occupied the north-west quarter of the walled town. Allectus and Marcus shared the duties of garrison commander and soon won over the wary natives and foreign merchants who hoped for a less tyrannical administration. They had the bearing of officers whose preference was for law and order, as opposed to the random bullying and theft by the now departed Trinovantes clan.

"I am pleased to find the place where the provincial governor once ruled this island in such good repair," Constantine oozed over their celebratory evening meal.

"God has willed it, my lord," Guithelin cheerfully replied. "In my dreams I saw your coming as a Godly and just ruler to bring order to this land..."

"Or perhaps my brother, Aldrien?" Constantine interrupted, dryly, winking at Allectus.

"The face was obscure, my lord, only the grace and might of a just hand was apparent. This was my vision and my heart's desire." He tucked into the fine sweetmeats and pigeon breasts as laughter rang out, releasing the tensions of the day. In private, Constantine reflected that he was Lord of nothing, still a landless military leader, tenured by fractious chiefs whose flimsy alliance might crumble at any time.

A CRY WENT up at the sight of a fleet of a dozen ships slipping menacingly along the Tamesis as far as the Roman bridge, their dragon heads edging past startled merchant boats that tried to steer away. They lowered their sails and ran out their oars in a practised manoeuvre, rowing against the flow of the dirty brown river, following the lead ship along the centre channel. The drawbridge was down, preventing the single mast ships from passing under the bridge and forcing them to beach their vessels on the shingle shore outside the town walls. Soon helmeted warriors leapt from their ships, shouting war cries and banging their weapons on their shields to announce their arrival. Horn blasts from the towers called the guards to their posts.

Allectus and Marcus, barely a week into their tenure as
Commanders of the Guard, met on the parapet over the south
gatehouse. They looked down on scurrying families who had
abandoned their pots, baskets and fishing nets to take to the
wooden planks that floated above the river mud and led to the
safety of the raised bridge approach.

"It seems our coming was timely," Allectus growled, seeing
the scampering traders on the bridge whipping their pigs and
goats into a trot.

But for Marcus it seemed time was suspended as he stared
down at the tide of frightened folk cramming through the gates,
his white-knuckled grip on the stone turret betraying his anxiety.
To his left, Allectus was barking out orders as guards scurried
past him. The Saxons swaggered across the mudflats with steely
menace, shouting in their harsh, guttural language. Two raiders
dragged a cowering boy from the first wicker hut they
encountered and, whilst their accomplices mocked the
wretched child's screams, butchered him as if he were no more
than an animal.

Marcus's glazed expression and dream-like state had not
gone unnoticed. "Your enemy has returned, Marcus," Allectus
intoned, slapping him on the shoulder and jolting him out of his
daze. "We shall lock them outside for now, but the bridge and
south bank settlement are exposed."

"I have a troop of fifty men stationed in the south bank
guardhouse," Marcus groaned, staring helplessly across the now
deserted bridge.

"They must buy time by raising the south arm of the
drawbridge to prevent these dogs from rushing over the bridge

to a feast of merry slaughter," Allectus replied. "We have nearly two thousand men in barracks, and five hundred horses. I estimate their numbers at barely five hundred."

Marcus eyed the more experienced commander as he marshalled his thoughts, struggling to shut out a living nightmare of guttural chanting in time to drum beats drifting on the wind. His fingers curled around the dragon medallion that hung from his neck, comforting him. "I shall send a rider across the bridge with an order to raise it and hold firm."

"Do it," Allectus growled. "And I shall order our cavalry to be mounted and ready by the north gate. If we draw them onto the firm meadow to the east, we can attack them by horse and send our soldiers out through the east gate."

Marcus ran to the ladder and swiftly descended, calling out for Quintus, his deputy, who was in the square, amidst a throng of activity, holding the reins of Marcus's horse. He fired urgent instructions and instantly Quintus mounted the horse and forced his way through the tide of frightened people coming through the gate, then galloped along the raised wooded walkway leading to the bridge. The Saxons had not yet reached the bridge approach and he passed unhindered to the centre. By now archers were firing arrows at any Saxons foolish enough to come too close to the walls. The milling warriors responded like trained dogs to a horn blast that called them to congregate on the foreshore to await a briefing from their leaders.

The veteran legionary dismounted and spoke hurriedly to the guards who controlled the drawbridge mechanism. "We must leave the north drawbridge down and go to the south side. We have to raise the south bridge. By leaving one side down, the gap will be too wide for our foe to jump across, but too narrow for a ship to pass through. Cut the ropes!"

Marcus watched on from the gatehouse parapet, concerned to see a group of fifty-or-so Saxon warriors detach themselves from the main body and stride purposefully towards the bridge.

Quintus had barely finished his briefing when wild shouts drew their attention to a horde of flaxen-haired warriors rushing towards them from the north bridge approach. Quintus led his horse across the divide with six others, whilst four guards hacked with their swords at the ropes that raised the bridge. This done, they rushed after their comrades and Quintus shouted the order to raise the south side of the drawbridge. Howling warriors threw axes at the wooden barrier before them, the gap of fifteen yards too wide to leap over. Quintus ordered crates to be brought so that archers could stand and fire arrows over the top of the bridge at the enraged enemy.

"We must draw them away from the bridge and south gate towards the east," Allectus said, dragging his steely gaze from the melee and leaning over the wall to survey the ground outside Londinium. The south side was clear of settlements but, in the year since the Romans had gone, wooden shacks and animal pens had been allowed to spring up on the east, west and north sides. These were now easy targets for the Saxons, although they had been abandoned and the livestock driven through the town gates for safety.

"An enticement, perhaps?" Marcus said, looking hopefully at the taller man.

Allectus paused before responding. "We could feign an escape through the east gate. The Saxons will go in pursuit and…"

"…be attacked by our riders waiting behind the north wall." Marcus caught the drift of his comrade's idea and they briefly sifted options until he said decisively, "Yes, that must work. They are ever hungry for blood and plunder. I shall remain here to marshal the defence of the walls."

"Then let me waste no time in riding to the barracks and assembling our cavalry. May your gods protect you." Allectus gripped Marcus's forearm, encouraging him with a grimace that cracked his scarred face.

A SOLDIER IN full armour could trot from the south gatehouse to the fort in the north-west corner of the enclosed town in twenty minutes, past stone and brick buildings clustered around the Forum, over the Wal Brook Bridge, and on past clusters of animal pens and wooden shacks in the outer extremities. On this day Allectus was glad of his horse, as he had to force his way past agitated townsfolk, milling livestock and anxious farmers looking for under-used corrals.

He entered the gates of the Roman fort, the oldest part of the town, laid out like a military camp with even rows of wooden barrack blocks, stables, a mess hall and a small commanders office. It was here that he found Prince Constantine.

"Ah, Allectus, come and join our briefing," Constantine said, his stern look briefly flirting with a smile. He was wearing a long white gown under a red cloak and had clearly come in haste from his morning bath.

"My lord, I am from the south wall. Marcus has taken charge of the defences and the Saxon hordes sit outside on the shoreline, making their plans. A detachment has stormed the bridge but has been held off by Quintus and fifty guards, who have half-raised the drawbridge and defend the south side."

Relief at his arrival was evident on the faces of the sub-commanders and Constantine.

"Your coming is timely, Allectus. Advise us. How should we proceed?"

"My lord, my briefing with Marcus has formulated a plan. The Saxons must be prevented from moving away to raid freely in the unguarded settlements around this town, as they surely will now they have seen the town is guarded. We must try to keep them together and draw them onto the east meadow where the land is flat and firm enough to use our horses."

"And how can we entice those bloodthirsty barbarians to enter the eastern meadow?" Constantine asked.

"By driving some cattle out of the east gate with a handful of our soldiers disguised as peasants in an act of escape. Then our cavalry can be waiting unseen behind the north wall. I believe it is worth a try." His eyes shone brightly at the prospect, and no one doubted him.

"Let it be done," Constantine said. "I will lead the cavalry and you may lead your peasant deserters." Allectus nodded and quickly barked out orders to his sub-commanders. An optio with a quickly-scribbled order from Constantine was dispatched to requisition two dozen head of cattle and drive them to the east gate. Preparations were made, and Constantine hurried to his Roman Governor's villa to be clad by his servant in military leather and chainmail.

Allectus led his men at a trot through the town centre, past the fountain and Imperial stone buildings in the Forum full of gawping townsfolk, to the east gate.

"Remove your helmets and cover your armour with these sack-cloths. Keep your swords sheathed and carry staffs for driving the cattle." Allectus knew there was no time to lose and ordered the gates to be opened as soon as the cattle were in place. They drove them out through the shaded gatehouse into bright morning sunlight, the sun now visible over the wall of the forest some five hundred yards before them. They joined a well-worn track that ran parallel to the town walls and headed north. The remainder of his troops stood in readiness behind the closed east gates.

The north gates were opened, and Constantine led his Armorican guards and assorted Briton cavalry over a stone bridge and onto the start of the Watling Street. They turned to their right onto a dirt track that ran between wooden hovels and a cemetery. Constantine wrinkled his nose in disdain at ravaged graves and tombs of wealthy citizens, looted by grave robbers and scavenged by dogs, leaving bones and torn rags strewn across the bare, compacted earth.

"There is no peace for the dead on this cursed island," one of the Armorican optios commented. They trotted east, towards the climbing sun, and stopped before the north-east tower. Constantine ordered a scout to dismount and creep forward to glance around the corner and keep watch for the cattle drovers and Saxon pursuers.

On the south wall, Marcus noticed the Saxons move off towards the east and moved along the parapet to the south east tower to watch their progress. "Archers follow me!" he yelled. On the tower platform he could see the cattle drovers to his left, now being pursued by hundreds of hooting and hollering Saxons. The sight of the swaggering Saxons, moving like a hungry wolf pack in time to a steady drum beat, made him shiver - but his soldier's instincts cut through his dread. "Archers, move along the east wall and wait for my command!"

The trap was set, and the confident Saxons marched into it. In truth, they were looking for a fight, and now they had one. The east gate opened and hundreds of men in armour rushed their middle section. The archers fired down on the Saxon stragglers. Once the cattle had been driven beyond the north-east corner, Allectus and his men threw off their sack-cloths and faced the enemy. Constantine fixed his black gaze on a target and slammed down his raised sword, leading his cavalry into a full charge. Townsfolk flocked to the east wall and cheered on their soldiers as archers picked off any Saxons who strayed too close to the wall.

The cavalry charge took the Saxons completely by surprise, and they soon realised they were in a fight for their lives. Saxon traders had seen Mandubracius's Londinium, ruled by ill-prepared and squabbling Britons, but the raiders now faced an entirely unexpected enemy. Axes, spears and swords hacked and slashed; the cries of wounded men and horses and the groans of the dying filled the air. Townsfolk on the wall cheered on their champions – it was a better spectacle than the tawdry games put on in the town's amphitheatre. In barely an hour it was over. The Saxons had been slaughtered and even the few who attempted to run back to their boats were intercepted by Quintus and the guards from the south bank, who blooded their blades on the men from the east. Only a handful were spared to be bound and paraded through the streets of Londinium by the gloating victors, before giddy and grateful townsfolk.

Chapter Six

CONSTANTINE ENSURED NEWS of the crushing victory over a mighty Saxon army spread across the land by sending out a host of messengers to every town. The proclamation, signed 'Constantine, Dux Bellorum', also called for all chiefs to attend a celebratory feast in Londinium at the next full moon.

"My dear Guithelin, your vision is only part-fulfilled," he said to the diminutive bishop in his private chamber. "This island needs a king, as recent events have shown. The people are content, knowing they have good governance and a well-trained army to defend them."

Guithelin smiled and replied, "That suggestion may be opposed by the chiefs of the bigger tribes who have power and ambition to grow their lands…"

"Yes," Constantine interrupted, "that is why YOU must propose it, and I will feign surprise." He poised a flagon of wine over the bishop's empty goblet and raised a questioning brow. Guethelin nodded. "Good. We will need chiefs ready to back us, of course. That is our most pressing task. Let us identify chiefs who can be swayed to welcome a King Constantine," he said, and then tipped the flagon for the open-mouthed cleric.

"Do you mean pay them?" Guithelin asked innocently.

"I mean we first identify them, then use our intelligence to decide how we might improve their situation. This may be by gifts of gold and silver."

"Or what else?"

"We must uncover their heart's desire and do what we can to satisfy it. Weapons, training, the construction of bridges or halls. A marriage alliance, maybe." He paused to slake his thirst.

After a moment's silence, Guithelin said, "My lord, this is politics and I feel somewhat uncomfortable..."

"You cannot say you want something and then complain about the means of getting it!" Constantine shouted, rattled by this man whose subtle interrogation brought to mind his saintly older brother, King Aldrien. "This may well be politics, dear Bishop, but we are both set on a course and must do all we can to succeed. I do not advocate murder or mischief, merely the building of support based on mutual interest. Will you help me in this?" He fixed his black eyes on the shrinking holy man who squirmed before giving his answer.

"Very well, my lord, I shall assist you in matters of intelligence. But this scheme has an ungodly whiff about it and the deal-making must be yours alone." Knowing so much, he had stood up to the Prince as much as he dared.

"Alright! I anticipated your reluctance, and so you and I will formulate the strategy and my commanders, Allectus and Marcus, shall make the visits. Before then, I propose a raid on Camulodenum to seize Mandubracius and recover the Roman riches he has plundered. Both will come in use."

Guethelin, squeezing his wrist, meekly acknowledged the plan. "My lord."

A MONTH LATER, chiefs, their families and guards began to arrive at Londinium. Temporary shelters had been constructed and army tents set up in guarded meadows outside the east and west walls to accommodate the volume of visitors. Shanty settlements close to the walls had been cleared and those displaced with skills or trades rehoused within the town. Constantine's engineers had been busy with improvements, including the establishment of a cattle market and warehouses where merchants could rent space. Livestock pens were concentrated in one quarter and kept separate from living quarters. Bishop Guithelin had his wish granted to take over the temple of Mithras and convert it to a Christian church that could accommodate a growing congregation.

"My lord," Guithelin puffed, running through the Imperial Senate building beside the striding prince. "I have an interesting proposition from a powerful chief to bring to you."

Constantine stopped suddenly and, under the indifferent gaze of Jupiter, looked down on the fawning bishop. "Leave us!" he yelled at his clerks, who scurried to their offices located behind doors along the marble-floored corridor.

"What is it?"

"I have just come from welcoming a powerful noble of the Coritani tribe, Severus Senovara, who would make a most powerful ally."

"What part of Britannia is he from and what would make him a willing ally?"

"He is the master of the former Roman garrison town of Lindum. It was a regional centre for tax collection, known as Britannia Flavia, and commands the middle part of this island. He is a man of great wealth and influence, and I understand he is looking for a suitable match for his daughter..."

"I see," Constantine said, stroking his pointed beard. "Is it your opinion that he is one of the most powerful men on this island?"

"Indeed, he is, my lord, and a Christian with the highest Roman manners. He is unlike the other rough native chieftains and maintains the Roman ways for the betterment of his people."

"Then I should meet him before our council. You may invite Severus Senovara and his household to my table this evening. There is still much to be done before tomorrow's council meeting. Find Allectus and Marcus and send them to me."

"It shall be done, my lord." Guithelin bowed and hurried off – down the marble steps of the tall Senate building and into his enclosed litter, to be carried by the four servants he employed to transport him through the streets of the busy town.

CAGED NIGHTINGALES SANG a welcome to Chief Severus Senovara as he entered the dining room that was once used by the Roman Governor to receive important guests. Painted murals covered the walls, depicting scenes from Greek and Roman mythology in their fading glory, and the gods of Olympus looked down approvingly from the high vaulted ceiling.

Severus's tanned face broke into a warm smile under white, close-cropped hair. "Prince Constantine, it is a pleasure to finally meet the noble leader who put the dreaded Saxons to the sword!" The two toga-clad men embraced, and Constantine invited his six guests to sit facing his senior officials and officers across the table. He clapped his hands and attendants appeared carrying platters of fruits and meats and pitchers of wine and ale.

Constantine introduced his officials and then Severus did the same for his family.

"...and next to my wife, Octavia, is my eldest daughter, Justina," Severus announced, with pride. "I have only daughters, my lord," he added.

Constantine smiled at the blushing maiden. "I am pleased to receive you and your family, Chief Severus, for in truth, I have met very few in Britannia who can be named as being of noble birth." Polite laughter rippled around the table.

"May I ask if you have a wife, my lord?" Severus asked as he sat.

Constantine blinked, startled by such a direct question from one he had only just met. "I have not yet wed. I am the younger brother to a king and have spent much of my life in the saddle, defending the borders of his kingdom. I have not considered the matter, but feel my brother and his queen may have plans for me as they look to consolidate their lands." He said this whilst filling his plate. He then began to eat, a signal to his followers to do the same. Small conversations broke out across the table as Constantine and Severus traded questions to get the measure of each other.

THE GREAT HALL of the Basilica, where citizens of Rome once debated important provincial matters, slowly filled. A stream of chiefs and their attendants entered, passing lines of decaying Saxon heads displayed on spikes at the entrance to the building and progressing through the wide double doors into a cooler space. They continued between rows of chairs and benches, through a great hall lit by oil lamps on Greek columns, to a raised dais where the chiefs were introduced to Prince Constantine. Bishop Guithelin announced their names and seated them.

Deals had continued to be brokered through the night and into the early morning, and it was agreed by that Constantine would look surprised at being proclaimed King, even if no one would wholly believe it. Guithelin hushed the audience of over one hundred and read a prepared statement introducing Prince Constantine and stating the purpose of his own mission, stressing the fact that he had taken it upon himself, guided by visions from God, to travel to the court of King Aldrien of Armorica to plead with him to come to the aid of Britannia.

Disturbing dreams had shown him Britannia facing internal strife and savage raiders from without. Prince Constantine was sent by his brother and had been welcomed by Valorian, Chief of the Atrebates, and other local chiefs, who had charged him with the defence of the south of Britannia. This had proved timely in view of the recent raid on Londinium. There were nods of assent and noises of approval from the assembled group of chiefs who had come from as far as the Wall of Hadrian to the north and the wilds of Dyfed to the west. The most powerful chiefs had been seated near the front, as their support would prove vital.

Constantine took to his feet, silencing the mutterings. "My noble chiefs, I thank you for your warm welcome. I believe this is the largest gathering of the nobility of Britannia since the Romans departed more than a year past, and I am pleased it has happened in a moment of celebration, following the defeat of a vicious and determined enemy by a combined force of Briton warriors, from many tribes, and my own Armorican guard."

He paused to encourage applause and stamping of feet. "I am also pleased to have made a good friend in Chief Valorian of the Atrebates who welcomed us to his town of Calleva Atrebatum, named by the Romans for his tribe, and who now rightly rules over that place. Indeed, life continues after the Romans' withdrawal and Briton tribes are reclaiming their birth right. This is good. I wish only to serve you as your military leader until such a time as my brother, King Aldrien, recalls me to his court."

Murmurs broke out and he stood quietly, assessing the mood of the audience. Valorian, seated at the front, had not noticed his exiled younger brother, Vortigern, creep into the back of the hall. A succession of chiefs took to their feet to ask Constantine to stay and pledge support with warriors. Finally, Severus stood and hushed the noise.

"My fellow chiefs, having heard this debate, I am now of a mind to invite Prince Constantine to be more than a 'Dux Bellorum', who may leave our shores at any time, and be our king of Britannia."

Uproar broke out, with shouts of 'Aye' from those in favour and some angry shouts of opposition. Constantine remained seated, maintaining an impassive expression, as Guithelin stood on the dais and attempted to restore order.

"Your proposal is an excellent one, Chief Severus of the Coritani, and perhaps the only way we can maintain peace and prosperity in our island. We have heard from Prince Constantine that he may, at any time, be recalled to Armorica by his brother, King Aldrien. Perhaps the only way we may keep him on our island to lead the fight against invaders is to make him our king, and by doing so elevate him to the same rank as his brother."

Severus remembered his lines, coughed, and continued, "You are right, dear bishop, and your guidance from God Almighty has delivered us to this point. I now make the offer of my daughter, Justina, in marriage to the noble Prince Constantine, to cement his bond with our island and forge a new royal dynasty!"

Again, this met with a mixed reaction, but Constantine noted that more appeared to be in favour than were against. Arguments broke out between neighbours as those not privy to the plot wondered what situation would be most advantageous to them.

"We have just come out from under the yoke of the Romans – why would we want a new king?" one shouted. "Conspiracy!" yelled another. Rumblings of agreement rippled through the hall, stoked by angry jeers from Vortigern, who identified the dissidents and moved closer to them.

Constantine took to his feet and raised his arms for silence. "My noble chiefs, your offer interests me. Indeed, it is my belief this island has no history before the Romans of being united under one king. You must realise that without the protection of the Roman legions or my brother's army your tribal lands will be exposed. And you should know, barbarians now threaten you from all sides. But if you are agreed, I would accept your offer to be king and take the hand of the noble Lady Justina in marriage, and I undertake to rule through a council of chiefs and respect your tribal lands and freedoms."

More mutterings broke out and he turned to nod to Allectus, who produced a bound prisoner from an anteroom and brought him forward. Constantine raised his arms for silence. "You see before you the noble Mandubracius, Chief of the Trinovantes, who opposed me in battle and was captured." This part of the performance elicited more shouts from the floor.

Constantine continued, "I now set him free, for his only crime was to oppose my coming to Londinium and sitting in his chair!" He cut the bonds of the bedraggled chief to roars of laughter. "My noble chiefs, if you are in agreement, I will charge Bishop Guithelin with convening a council of the ten most powerful chiefs in this land, including Chief Mandubracius, and let them meet to discuss this proposal. If I hear a majority shout 'Aye', then let it be done!" Constantine looked as regal as possible in his purple robe, leaning forward and jutting out his pointy black beard, as his eyes shone like burning coals whilst scanning the faces before him.

A loud chorus of 'Aye!' rang around the hall, drowning out a few dissenting voices. Constantine bowed and withdrew to his private rooms, leaving Guithelin to take charge of the arrangements. After thirty minutes Guithelin reported to Constantine that ten chiefs had agreed to sit together that afternoon and discuss the matter of being ruled by King Constantine. Seven of those, including Mandubracius, had already agreed terms with Constantine, or his representatives, for their support.

"Power lies where men believe it to lie," Constantine quipped happily, pouring wine for his supporters. "They see in me a noble prince of a noble and powerful family. It is but a short journey from there to see me as their king."

Chapter Seven

QUEEN JUSTINA SMILED benignly at the room of nobles who had gathered to see her baby son, Julius. A year had passed since both her wedding and the coronation of Constantine as King of Britannia elevated her to the position of Queen. She now passed the baby wrapped in a finely woven blanket to her courtly ladies who cooed at the bawling infant. This freed Justina to greet the line of waiting nobles and offer her hand to be kissed.

She was revered by her people who proudly identified with the beautiful and eloquent Briton. She trod delicately on golden sandals, wearing a finely-woven white woollen mantle, belted at the waist with a cord of gold that was studded with silver coins displaying the heads of long-gone emperors, drawing the admiring glances of men and women alike to her fine figure. Her nut-brown hair was plaited and tied with purple cords and crowned with a band of fine calfskin twisted like rope. She pulled at a silver cuff inscribed with her tribal motif of two stags fighting as she glided gracefully along the line. Her robes, fluttering in a slight breeze, were held together with delicate fibulas cast in silver and set with brightly-coloured gemstones in an elegant blending of Roman and Briton fashion.

"You are most welcome to Londinium, my cousin Freda," she said to a muscular woman with pale yellow ponytails hanging over her shoulders.

"My queen, you are an inspiration to all Briton women."

"I hear you understand the Saxon tongue, after your father?" Justina asked her.

"I learned a little at his knee, my lady."

"Then we will have use of you in our court as there are many traders and soldiers seeking employment from your father's land."

"I am willing to stay and be your companion, my queen, and speak with the Saxons on your behalf. I can also fight with a sword and throw a spear," the taller woman added, standing up to her full height.

Justina laughed and replied, "Then I will make you my guard and attendant."

"VORTIGERN HAS FLED north, my lord, with a group of rebellious nobles, beyond the reach of our allies." Allectus had returned to Londinium after three months pursuing rebel chiefs who opposed Constantine's coronation.

Constantine scowled his displeasure. "You will address me as 'Your Majesty' from now onwards. And what of Marcus? I see you have returned without him." The former Governor's hall had been transformed into his throne room, its Roman influence reduced by a series of tapestries hanging over the murals, which depicted hunting scenes. His own banner, a joining together of his hawk motif flying above the queen's doe, hung behind his raised dais.

"He asked your leave to return with his men to Calleva, Your Majesty, to ensure the safety of that town and the lands of Chief Valorian. With your permission he will remain there and resume his duties as Commander of the South and West."

"This is not seeking my permission. He has defied me by not returning with you to report."

A broody silence fell between the two men whilst Constantine stroked his beard. "Continue with your briefing. What resistance did you meet with?"

"We did raid the village of a troublesome chief in Prima, at the instigation of your father-in-law, Severus, Your Majesty. He was captured and hanged, his goods seized and his sons delivered to Severus as slaves."

"My father was not slow to use your might to settle his local quarrels," Constantine smirked, signalling an attendant to bring ale. He stood and walked to his banqueting table, affording his commander a sight of his growing paunch, and indicated Allectus should sit. The two men drank, and Constantine's mood lightened. "You have done well, Allectus, but it worries me that there is a group of rebels north of Hadrian's Wall plotting mischief. For every chief there are plenty of disgruntled brothers and cousins who want land and titles."

"This is true everywhere, Your Majesty. We have a good support base of the most powerful chiefs and their sons must be kept at your court, but they must respect you and fear your army, otherwise it will drip away like the morning dew." They drank and Allectus admired the tapestries that had come from Armorica. "Your family banners look well in this hall," he added between gulps. "I pray you are not angry with Marcus – he is a valuable ally and was anxious to see his wife and family, Your Majesty. The blame is mine for assenting to his request – we are now like brothers."

The two men eyed each other before Constantine managed a smirk. "I am not angry. He is a most valued commander and a bridge between us and these troublesome Britons. I can see that you form a formidable team. I also have news - a son, Allectus, a boy prince named Julius." The two men clashed goblets and drank the good health of the baby.

"This is a good sign, Your Majesty, and cements your position as ruler of this land. By your leave, I shall meet your Commander of the Guards, Quintus, for a briefing. With your permission, I shall remain here and send him out with the supply wagons to evaluate our eastern shore forts." Allectus sat back and regarded his King. Ever since the Saxon assault on Londinium, he had taken a more direct approach with his military advice, sensing his influence had grown in importance with his master. He could see a softening in Constantine, and the plumpness of a fattened partridge - no doubt the effects of a fairly untroubled first year of kingship, and the positive influence of the queen. "The Queen is much loved in this land, Your Majesty," he added.

"And what of me?" Constantine abruptly asked, jerking his head to fix his raptor's eyes on Allectus.

"They love and respect you, my king. You are seen as a godly and noble leader, with great wisdom and military might that was lacking in this land. I have heard few dissenters on my travels."

"You are a wise and faithful adviser, Allectus. You shall remain by my side. I have missed your forthright and honest words - we have much to discuss."

Allectus rose to take his leave, but Constantine looked up suddenly and raised a pointed finger. "Ah, one more thing,

Allectus – how could I have forgotten? Your wife, Adair, and your son have arrived from Armorica on the last supply ship. They await you in your quarters."

IN CALLEVA, MARCUS found a busy and prospering town, and a pensive chief in Valorian.

"Pray, tell of your adventures with Allectus in the North," Valorian said, indicating that Marcus should sit at his table.

"My lord, we did fight a number of skirmishes with rebellious chiefs, but these were small affairs that were done in a matter of minutes. Our might and resolve soon quashed all resistance."

"And what news of my brother, Vortigern?"

Marcus paused as he drank from his goblet. "We followed his trail to the northern town of Eboracum. There he evaded us by riding north before our arrival. We understand he travels with a group of six nobles – none are chiefs, mainly brothers and cousins of chiefs who hold grievances, my lord. They have no more than a hundred men following them."

Valorian leaned forward as he listened, fixing his eyes on Marcus. "This is a dangerous group indeed," he muttered.

"Aside from settling a dispute for the queen's father, Severus, our most important meeting was with Chief Getterix of the powerful Brigantes tribe at Eboracum. He had sent one of his sons to attend the council meeting and the king's coronation, but he had stubbornly remained in the north. Getterix reminded us that he is descended from Queen Cartimandua. As you know, their tradition is to be independent rulers of their lands whilst co-operating with the former occupying legions of Rome. On this basis, he swore fealty to King Constantine. He controls the North up to the Wall and has over five thousand warriors at his call."

"Did he offer to capture my brother and the other rebels?"

"He did, my lord, however…"

"What?" Valorian's eyes narrowed.

"Allectus felt, after the meeting, that he is cautious and unwilling to act on the King's behalf. I also had that feeling, my lord. I expect nothing will happen."

Valorian ground his teeth in frustration. "My brother is ambitious and will make an alliance with the Devil to get the power he craves. We have not heard the last of this."

Once outside the busy Basilica, Marcus strode past stalls that lined the outside walls of the Forum. He breathed in the fragrance of herbs and grinned at two young sellers in dispute, not old enough for bumfluff on their chins, but drawing the attention of passers-by like veteran traders. He stopped outside a temple to buy a finely crafted pot that bore a dragon motif, dropping a couple of small coins into the grubby hand of an elderly woman. The Defender of Calleva smiled benevolently and acknowledged the bows of townsfolk as he strode towards his villa, whistling as he passed through a wrought iron gate in the side wall of the barracks block and nodding at a startled sentry who stood to attention.

He found Cordelia standing in the shade of the terrace, watching their son, Uther, and adopted son, Brian, splashing in the fountain. She cried out as Marcus marched into the courtyard and rushed towards him. Soon Marcus was surrounded by his family, including his eight-year-old daughter,

Esther. "My, the children are growing," he laughed, rubbing their hair and picking up the lively toddler, Uther, and swinging him around. Turning to his left he noticed his deputy commander, Drustan, hovering next to a pillar.

"I shall meet with you shortly, Drustan, in my office. First, I'll wash off the dust of travel and spend some time with my dear ones."

Drustan stood to attention and banged his forearm across his chest, leaving the Pendragon family to their happy reunion.

An hour later the patient Drustan made his report to his commander. "I escorted Queen Nathair back to her village without incident, Sir. Then we heard reports that a Jute raiding party had besieged Portus Adurni. I led a troop of fifty men to that fort and we did find two boats and about sixty warriors loitering beyond the range of Portus Adurni's archers. They had burned the settlement by the shore and chased off the inhabitants. We did fight them, our force swelled by men from the fort. We killed about half their number and the rest escaped in one of the boats."

Marcus listened in silence to the report, visions of the Saxon assault on Londinium playing in his head. "You have done well, Drustan. I fear these raids will be regular trials during the seasons of fair weather."

"Aye, they have a base on the Isle of Vectis and I hear their numbers grow. They are a plague that has no cure, except good steel." He drew his gladius and slapped the blade on his open palm. Marcus grinned and invited him to sit and share a jug of wine. They were young men in their twenties who were already veterans in the bitter business of war.

"There is nothing for it except to send out regular patrols. How are our stocks of food?"

"We have been blessed with a good harvest of wheat and barley, and Chief Valorian's men collect tithes of crops and livestock on our behalf, from surrounding farms and from traders in the marketplace. We are well-stocked, sir. The freed Roman slaves who joined our defence have remained with us and keep the soldiers in good order."

"Good. And what of the men?"

"We remain with a standing garrison of one hundred and fifty, sir. Most have now seen some action and are more seasoned soldiers for having dipped their swords and spears in Saxon blood."

"And have the people accepted Constantine as their king?" He eyed the weathered face of his deputy closely.

"Aye, sir. There is acceptance and contentment amongst the people. They rejoiced at the news of your victory over the Saxons at Londinium and feel safer for it."

Marcus drank and stared up at a wooden chandelier holding six bronze oil lamps that was suspended from the ceiling by a rope tied off on a wall bracket. "I will write a letter to our neighbouring chiefs that you must learn and recite to them, stating our current situation and our need for more young warriors to join us. You will ride south and west to Venta Bulgarum and then further west to the coastal fortress of Isca Dumnoniorum. Find out what you can about who is there and how many men they have."

"I will send a messenger to you from Isca," Drunstan said.

Marcus nodded. "Then go north along the Roman road to Lindis and Aquae Sulis. From there to Glouvia, and across the Severna River to Isca Silurum. On your return you shall pass through Corinium. I am anxious to know the situation in these places now ruled by tribal clans."

Drustan drained his pewter mug, stood, saluted his commander and left Marcus to his quiet reflection. Marcus would remain in Calleva and enjoy the company of his family until it all began again with a summons from his king, or news of determined raiders spilling onto the south coast.

Chapter Eight

STEADY DRIZZLE ACCOMPANIED the line of silent riders on a coastal path where sky and sea blended into an unwelcoming wall of grey away to their left. The sodden warriors covered their heads as best they could with animal hides or cloaks and sat hunched in their saddles, allowing their mounts to follow the horse before them. Vortigern called a halt on a high bluff above a fishing settlement. After a few brief words with the two warrior leaders accompanying him, he watched the deadly host descend on the village with murderous intent.

He followed slowly, then sat alone outside the village as the cries of helpless victims filled the air. They did not run, just cowered and accepted their fate. He reflected on ten years spent in exile – in part, north of The Wall with vulgar Picts, but more latterly in the mountains of North Gwynedd as a guest of King Cunedda. The powerful king was no ally of King Constantine and made it clear when Allectus came visiting that he would defend his borders against them. Allectus had not returned.

Now Vortigern, a man approaching thirty years, led an army that numbered one thousand warriors - half men of Gwynedd under Cunedda's son, Lugus, and half a force of hired swords made up of Britons, Gauls and Saxons who called themselves 'Gwessians' after the place from where their leader, Bran, hailed. A warrior waved to him that it was safe to enter, and he spurred his horse to a slow walk towards the centre of the settlement, past miserable wretches, their wrists bound, kneeling in the mud, awaiting an unknown fate.

"We need camp followers, Bran," he said to the blood-splattered warrior panting heavily near him. "Do not kill them all."

LONDINIUM HAD GROWN as a centre of commerce where merchants from Gaul and beyond plied their trade with locals, bartering expertly woven cloth, tailored garments, leather shoes, polished gemstones, salted meat and barrels of fish in exchange for painted pots, animal furs, brooches and necklaces fashioned from silver, and the produce of the land. King Constantine and Queen Justina had watched it grow and had encouraged traders to prosper with their patronage. A second son, Aurelius, had been born two years after Julius and, six years on, baby Constans had arrived. The princes further strengthened the prospect of a ruling dynasty and peace across the land, despite the ever-present threat of summer raids that kept them all in a state of readiness to flee or resist.

It was a restless urge one mild day that prompted Justina to take her oldest sons to the senate where she knew the tedium of his routine would be trying her husband.

Aurelius ran to his father, waving a wooden sword. Constantine laughed and helped the energetic boy to kneel beside him on his huge oak throne. "My feisty son. You shall be the warrior prince who shall protect this kingdom."

"Yield!" shouted Aurelius, lifting the point of his toy sword towards his father's throat, but he was the one to yield when his father waved it away and prodded his son's ribs.

Constantine glanced at his eldest son, Julius, standing awkwardly to one side with his tutor, clutching a wax tablet to his chest on which he had been practising his letters. Beckoning him closer, he spoke not ungently to him. "Julius, you shall one day be king and must have knowledge to be fair and wise. But you must also be strong, so that your subjects will respect you. For without respect, your words will be greeted with scorn. That is why it is my will that you spar daily with Quintus, learning to fight with sword, spear and shield." He frowned at the nut-brown hair hanging limply from the bowed head above a pair of bony white shoulders. "And do not let me hear again that you have been missing these lessons."

Justina walked up to her eldest son and lifted his chin with her hand. "Do not sulk, dear Julius. Even a boy named for Rome's greatest general must mind his father's word."

"Yes, mother," Julius whispered.

"And we will have the reverse problem with his one," Constantine laughed, putting Aurelius down and watching him charge out of the room as if going to war, trailed by his maid. Julius and his tutor were more dignified in their leave-taking.

"You must rest, my lord," Justina cooed, stroking her husband's arm as he shifted uncomfortably on his throne. "Your legs appear heavy today, and you must drink the potion prepared by your physician to alleviate the swelling…"

"Stop fussing woman!" He groaned, lifting his right leg to place it on a stool. "I shall deal with the petitioners waiting outside, then I will return to the villa and rest." He had become overweight and irritable, rarely venturing out from the close confines of the basilica building and his villa, connected by a footpath through an enclosed garden to the rear of the imperial building. The complex had been built for the safety of the

Provincial Governor, by Romans still mindful of the slaughter and destruction inflicted by Queen Boudicca of the Icenii barely thirty years before the town walls and buildings had been constructed. Some four hundred years had passed since then, and the Imperial town had been maintained in good order.

"Then I shall take the boys to the port to watch the ships. It is their favourite thing. We shall meet in the evening for prayers with Bishop Guithelin. May God bless you, my king." She kissed him lightly on the cheek and withdrew through the rear corridor to the gardens. Spring had come after a mild winter and she rejoiced at the songs of birds and the dances of butterflies around the heads of Roman emperors who lined her path.

AT THE LIGHTLY-GUARDED east gate, a cart loaded with firewood, escorted by four cloaked men, entered through the shaded gatehouse. They nodded at a disinterested guard and led their horse towards the livestock pens where they were directed. Bran removed his hood and looked in wonder at the two-storey townhouses, joined together in rows that lined the straight cobbled streets. Washing hung above their heads on lines strung between balconies on which children played with their minders. He had seen the Roman town of Viroconium, near his village in Gwynedd, but it was merely a legionaries' fort and nothing like this.

"This is a fine place of Roman manners," he whispered to a comrade, the crunch of their wheels adding to an unfamiliar cacophony of sounds. Once out of sight of the gate guards they drove their cart into a side lane and rummaged amongst the wood for their weapons and armour.

NATHAIR CURSED HERSELF that her heart still ached after so many years. The joy of finding first love in the arms of the muscular Allectus had filled her dreams and infused her waking reflections, driving out all prospects of happiness and feeding a growing hatred for the man who had stolen her passion. She had refused all offers of marriage and had remained childless, indifferent to the hopes of her clan for an alliance and an heir. A pang of deep desire stabbed at her heart on seeing the man she loved striding in a carefree manner, his toga hiding the powerful battle-scarred body she yearned for - but now only the bitterness of rejection remained to fuel her enmity. She had often thought of revenge but knew deep down that all she really wanted was to be with him again.

Nathair watched Allectus walking with his wife, Adair, on his arm, smiling and sharing confidences in their perfect world. Behind them skipped a boy, no more than ten years, holding a wooden toy of a Roman galley, making it rise and fall on imaginary waves. She had come to Londinium for the next council meeting of chiefs, not something she regularly attended, as her tribe were subordinate to the powerful Atrebates, represented by Valorian, but called upon to report on the worsening situation on the south coast.

Off to her left a commotion dragged her attention away from the promenading family. Cries, shouts, and the faint sound of swords clashing caused her to reach for the dagger handle at her waist.

"My lady, there is fighting near the east gate. Come quickly to the villa for your protection!"

"No! I shall remain here. Bring me my sword." Below her Allectus was calmly escorting his wife and son towards stone steps that led to the rear gardens of villas reserved for those of high office. She waited patiently for five minutes, during which time townsfolk ran about screaming 'barbarians!' Once her armed guards had joined her with her sword and shield, she moved off in the direction that Allectus had gone.

"My lady, the Forum is this way!" her attendant cried.

"We are going that way. Follow me!"

Vortigern and Lugus had led their warriors in through the east gatehouse, once Bran and his men had killed the guards and opened the gates, and now fanned outwards into the streets, slashing and stabbing at the terrified occupants.

"Lugus, come with me – we must find King Constantine before the full guard is raised from the barracks." They drove their horses through crowded streets, bumping aside and slashing at anyone who crossed their path. In barely a minute they forced their way into the open space of the Forum and rode past a fountain, under Neptune's glare, towards the steps of the Basilica. They charged up the dozen stone stairs and clashed with the half dozen guards standing outside the double oak doors. The doors were barred to them, so Vortigern led them around the side of the building, scaling a low wall to gain entry to the gardens and hacking at startled clerks who ran for their lives. The side door was open, and the fifty-or-so warriors charged into the dimly lit interior.

"Search for the king!" Vortigern shouted, his instincts leading him down a corridor towards an elaborately-decorated door. "In here!" he yelled. Two burly Picts put their shoulders to the locked door and soon barged it open. Inside, ailing King Constantine cowered in a corner, surrounded by six guards with bristling swords pointing from behind ornate oval shields.

The guards fought fiercely in defence of their master, killing a number of Lugus's men, but they were soon overpowered as more screaming blue-painted warriors streamed through the door. Vortigern stood to one side until the guards had been killed and then, wasting little time on ceremony, grinned at the cringing black-eyed king. "No speeches left, my lord?" he mocked, before driving his sword into his victim's fat belly. As Constantine moaned and fell to his side, Vortigern grabbed the gold band from his hair. He pulled a bejewelled necklace over the dying man's head and removed a silver torque from his neck before cutting his throat. The last embers of life briefly flicked in Constantine's eyes as his ten-year reign came to a sudden and violent end.

"Come on – to the villas!" Vortigern yelled. They streamed out of the rear door of the building, pushing over statues of emperors as they converged on the gate that led to a path to the villas where Constantine's family and other dignitaries would be hiding. Vortigern knew the full might of the guards would be crossing the town from the barracks in the north-west corner and wanted to eliminate the royal family and their supporters as quickly as possible. He had planned his attack to the day after half of the guard had marched north, knowing that barely five hundred guards would be remaining in the town to man the walls and gates. He had calculated that his force of a thousand would be enough to defeat them and take the town, but first he must stop the queen and her sons from escaping.

ON RECEIVING REPORTS of the scale of the attack, Allectus had taken it upon himself to find Queen Justina and the princes and take them to the relative safety of the south gatehouse. They were protected by their bodyguards in their villa, and Allectus had no news for them of the king. He had assembled twelve soldiers as a guard and now led them, with Queen Justina, Adair, the three boys and baby strapped to a nurse behind him and between two ranks of soldiers. Their maids and attendants jogged behind, looking fearfully over their shoulders as the battle raged around them. The queen's kinswoman and bodyguard, Freda, brought up the rear, her golden braids swishing from side to side beneath a silver helmet as she scanned the buildings for sight of the enemy.

Queen Nathair and her guard of ten followed a short distance behind. She ordered her men to stop and they looked on from a raised footpath as Allectus and his group were attacked by a screaming horde of thirty-or-more warriors in the square before the south gatehouse.

"Shall we help them, my queen?" a guard asked.

"Not yet – let us wait…"

"Form a line and fall back slowly to the gatehouse!" Allectus yelled, his powerful voice booming above the din. More guards who had been fleeing before the attackers now turned and joined his line, as a shield wall of twenty now faced down the Gwessian assault. Bran, as powerfully built as Allectus, barged his way through his men and faced up to him. Allectus glanced back and was dismayed to see that Queen Justina, his wife and their sons were still not inside the relative safety of the stone guardroom.

"My queen! To the guardhouse!" he yelled, just as Bran rushed at him, swinging a huge two-handed battle axe at his head. Allectus raised his shield that shattered with the impact. He thrust at Bran with his sword but was off-balance and didn't pierce the man's thick leather vest. Bran clouted Allectus in the face with the butt of his axe and forced his way through the line, almost going down into the dust when it gave. Allectus staggered backwards but raised his sword to parry the next blow, his helmet having taken some of the impact. With the line broken, combat raged all around as Allectus, reeling, pursued Bran, who threw down his axe and unsheathed his sword. Bran, the son of King Cunedda, had the confidence of a champion, but had met his match in the unshakable self-belief and experience of Allectus. They traded blows as men fell about them, but Allectus had the disadvantage of worry. He glanced behind again and let his guard down, crying out in pain when slashed across his left bicep.

Nathair gasped at the sight of Allectus stumbling backwards under the blow of the axe and seemed to awake from a dream. "To battle!" she yelled and led her guards towards the rear ranks of the Gwessian mercenaries. Their screams tore into the air above the compacted earth running red with blood, the groans of the dying adding to the din in the square. Archers on the walls attempted to pick off those attackers who were on the fringes of the fighting, as Allectus and his dwindling group of guards fell back on the guardhouse.

The momentum was with the Gwessians and their blood was up. They were there for plunder, but first must eliminate all resistance. They drove the buckling guards backwards towards the gatehouse and managed to raise the spar, throwing open the double gates.

Allectus and the last of the men staggered through the door to the guardhouse and barricaded it against their enemy. His duel with Bran was unfinished, but he was too weak to continue and there were other pressing matters. He was blowing hard and bleeding badly from wounds to his arm and head.

"My queen, the day is not going well," he puffed as he was guided to a stool. "I fear the worst and you must flee to the harbour and take to ship."

"I cannot leave the king!" she wailed. Adair put her arm around Justina's waist to comfort her as the ashen faces of the boys looked up. Freda stood to one side, her face set in a look of defiance.

"I shall escort you with what men we have left, and you must all sail for Noviomagus and wait there for news…" He groaned and bent forward as Adair dabbed at his head wound with a damp cloth. "Half our guard is out on the road – perhaps they will come back and turn the tide in our favour. Until then, you must take the princes and go."

The sight of Nathair, with her flame-coloured hair, swinging her sword at the enemy had rallied a number of guards and townsfolk to her side, and they now drove the Gwessians out through the gates. Allectus and his half-dozen remaining soldiers emerged through the guardroom door and he locked eyes on Nathair. They had not seen each other in eight years, and now stood staring as others waited for orders.

"My lady…" he mumbled.

"There is no time. What would you have us do now, Commander of the Guard?" she asked, glaring through her rage. Adair was now standing beside her husband and her eyes met those of the fierce Regnii queen.

"We must escort the queen and the others to a ship. Will you help us?" Allectus moaned through gritted teeth. He tried to blink away the blur on his vision.

Nathair hesitated. "Form a guard for the queen!" she cried, turning away from Allectus and seeing her soldiers reinforced by a crowd of townsfolk armed with whatever weapons they had picked up. "We are Britons, and this is our land!" she yelled and was answered with raised weapons and shouts of defiance. "Follow me!"

Allectus watched her sweep before him through the gates, followed by both civilians and soldiers alike. He led his party out after them. The Gwessians had fanned out along the docks and were randomly attacking any unfortunates they encountered. They had become a rabble and seemed, to his eyes, to be without leadership.

"There," Allectus yelled, pointing to a merchant ship whose mast was up and was ready to sail. They jogged and stumbled towards the ship, Freda indicating with the tip of her sword a group of Gwessians who were moving towards them with menace. Together, Allectus's men, the volunteers and Nathair's guard faced up to the threat and fighting broke out. Amid the clamour, the royal party were ushered onto the wooden pier and towards the ship, now in the bustle of casting off.

"Hold, good sir!" Allectus shouted, stumbling towards the rocking boat. "The queen would board!" The looks of frightened sailors showed a reluctance to delay their departure. Allectus ordered his men to grab the ropes and heave the ship back in. "There is silver for you all. Give us your plank!" He briefly kissed his son and wife and urged them to follow the Queen onto the ship as fighting broke out around him. Freda led the Queen and her followers up the gangplank, startling the sailors who had not seen a woman warrior the size of a man. Allectus drew his sword and faced the onrushing enemy with the last of his men as the gangplank was withdrawn and the ship moved off into the current.

"Allectus!" Adair cried, seeing that her husband had not joined them.

The women and children looked on helplessly as their men fought for their lives, the boat now aided in its swift departure by a dozen eager oarsmen. Allectus had two men on him, one stabbing with a spear and another slashing with a sword. His parries and counter-thrusts were becoming slower as his strength ebbed and his blurred eyes betrayed him. He fell to his knees as the spear's tip entered between his ribs, and the sword hacked at his neck as he fell for the last time. Nathair screamed and rushed towards him, but it was too late. The Armorican commander lay dead on the quay as his wife sobbed and clutched her ashen son against her breast to shield him from the sight.

Nathair and her guard finished off the Gwessians on the pier and she dropped to one knee beside the body of her former lover. She ruffled his thick, tawny hair one last time, and removed a moonstone necklace from around his neck, replacing it with one of her own. It was a brief farewell as her guards shouted that more of the enemy were coming. Other Gwessians were looting ships along the harbour, but out through the gates more warriors came running.

"They are not ours," Nathair said. "Come, let us run to the bridge and make for the safety of the south side!" She noticed her maid was on her knees in the mud beside the pier. "Are you injured, Brenna?"

"No, my queen. The little prince is beneath the pier."

Nathair jumped down off the wooden platform and looked into the gloom. The scared face of eight-year-old Aurelius stared back. "Come boy, we must hurry," she commanded, and Aurelius took her hand. She pulled him out from the sticky mud and gave him to her strongest guard to carry. "Hurry - they will soon be upon us!" They ran towards the steps that took them onto the bridge approach and huddled with all their group of assorted soldiers and townsfolk on the bridge. Nathair nominated half a dozen to hang back and fight off their pursuers and led the rest towards the drawn-up drawbridge.

"Lower the bridge for the Queen of the Regnii!" her followers shouted at the terrified faces peeping around the side. They quickly complied and all, save the brave rear guard, crossed in safety.

QUEEN JUSTINA HUGGED Adair and a pale Julius as they wept over the death of brave Allectus and the loss of the town. Twists of smoke rose from behind the walls and small figures, like ants, ran along the bridge as the mayhem continued. Justina looked around her and saw the wet-nurse with baby Constans strapped tightly to her breast standing close by. "Where is Aurelius?" she cried. No one had noticed that her second son was missing. A quick search of the ship confirmed that neither he nor his maid were aboard.

Justina cried out in grief and tore at her hair. "Where is my boy? I have lost a husband and a son on this cursed day!" Freda stood awkwardly to one side, her face betraying her guilt at not noticing that the little prince was missing. The two bereft wives sobbed and held each other. They knew there was no going back. Their ship hugged the south bank of the ever-widening estuary, forming an unhappy convoy of fleeing merchant ships riding the growing sea swell of the Germanic Sea.

NATHAIR AND HER band, allied with the South Bank guard, held the bridge and waited until nightfall. It was clear to them that the town had been taken by wild raiders whom most seemed to think were Picts from north of The Wall. Others had seen many foreign fighters, including flaxen-haired Saxons, fighting in the enemy ranks.

She later sat with her Regnii attendants and the little prince in the guardhouse, all warming themselves by a fire in the hearth and sipping from mugs of ale to calm them.

"What happened to you, little prince, that you fell under the pier?" she asked Aurelius.

The shy boy, traumatised by the amount of violence he had witnessed, looked up at her with wide, fearful eyes. "My maid, Ailsa, was chopped down and she pushed me under the pier, my lady."

Nathair hugged him and ruffled his fair hair. "Then she was a faithful servant who died saving you. I will look after you,

Aurelius, until we know what has happened to your family. We have all lost someone close to us in this mad slaughter."

"Do you have children, my lady? Are they safe?"

"Bless you, child. I will have no children now but my people - but I do have a chirpy young nephew about your age called Verica."

The boy's eyelids began to droop and his head nodded, fighting sleep. She smiled and stroked his hair, thinking of Allectus and what might have been.

"Go with my maid - she will give you some broth and put you to bed. In the morning we shall learn more about what has happened to your noble father and our friends in the town. But sleep in peace, knowing that your mother and brothers have made good their escape. Go now, and goodnight." She kissed his forehead and watched him climb a wooden ladder, wondering what challenges lay ahead for the young prince.

THE END

EPILOGUE

Dearest Queen Justina,

It is with a heavy heart, but some slender jubilation, that I write this missive to you. Word has reached me that you did not tarry on our south coast and instead made the wise choice to flee to King Aldrien's court in Armorica. I have no doubt that you and your children will be safe there.

I have taken up refuge in Calleva, under the protection of noble Valorian. Our town of Londinium is now in the grip of Vortigern, who calls himself 'king'. He is no Christian and his pagan thugs hail from the remote places of Britannia and from the Saxon lands.

Your noble husband was villainously slain in his chambers by Vortigern - a mercifully quick end, dear lady, but I fear he was not accorded a Christian burial. He is in my prayers, as are you and your sons. Britannia was blessed to enjoy the peaceful and prosperous reign of Constantine. The spirited prince I first met, with God's grace, learned to be a stalwart ruler who is much lamented. My followers and I made a hasty retreat once the fate of Londinium was known.

But I do, at least, have some good news for you. Your second son, Prince Aurelius, was found in the mayhem of battle by Queen Nathair and she has conveyed him in safety to Calleva, where he has been taken into the home of Commander Marcus and his Christian wife, Cordelia. They have two boys of their own and Aurelius has settled in well with his new playmates.

I will see to the boy's education whilst I remain in Calleva, and Marcus has undertaken to keep the little prince's identity a secret until such a time as we can send him to you.

Until then, I remain your faithful servant in our Lord Jesus Christ,

Guithelin, Bishop of Londinium

In this Year of Our Lord, CDXX

AUTHOR'S NOTE

The abandonment of the Province of Britannia by the Romans took place over a number of years, leading to a final separation around the year 410 AD. It is in this year that a letter from the Emperor Honorius advised the last administrators that Britannia must 'look to its own defence'. The Roman legions had withdrawn incrementally over a number of years leading up to the final separation to bolster the defence of Gaul as a troubled Western Empire fought with itself and attacking Germanic tribes.

What happened next in Britannia is still the subject of conjecture and debate by historians and archaeologists who have few scraps of evidence to go on. The oral tradition of storytellers and some scant accounts by monks and Welsh chroniclers has left us with a tantalising glimpse of a desperate defence of the island from invaders, and the suggestion that tribal chiefs elected a high king or 'leader of battles' to lead their army. Resistance to the colonisation of what is now England by the Anglo-Saxons continued for approximately three hundred years, so we can assume there was some organised resistance by the Britons. Reliable record keeping began again around 887 with the Anglo-Saxon Chronicles in the reign of King Alfred the Great.

The story of Constantine, first king of post-Roman Britannia, is first told by Geoffrey of Monmouth in his *History of Kings of Britain* (*Historia Regum Britanniae*), written around the year 1136. Many historians have discounted this as an unreliable source due to the author's habit of supplementing 'facts' with 'invention'. He clearly was a man with a creative mind, but there is evidence that he had done his research and taken account of the writings of monks Gildas, Nennius, Bede, and the Welsh chroniclers - and some are now of the view that he may have had access to other source material that has not survived the passage of time.

Geoffrey of Monmouth also gives us the story of 'cruel tyrant' Vortigern and his subsequent battles with the sons of Constantine – Ambrosius Aurelianus and Uther Pendragon. In time, Uther becomes king and fathers King Arthur, but that is for another story…

More recently, Geoffrey's work has been re-examined by historian Miles Russell in his book, *Arthur and the Kings of Britain: The Historical Truths Behind the Myths*. He defends Geoffrey's seemingly haphazard approach and explains how individual elements can be traced back to the first century BC, a time when Britain was making first contact with Rome. Geoffrey of Monmouth's skill was to weave these early traditions together with material culled from post-Roman sources in order to create a national epic. In doing so, he also created King Arthur, a composite character whose real origins and context are detailed in Russell's book.

Russell argues that Geoffrey of Monmouth was no mere peddler of historical fiction but was a man whose painstaking research preserved the earliest foundation myths of Britain. Russell concludes that it is time to re-evaluate the *Historia Regum Britanniae* and shine a new light into the so-called 'Dark Ages'.

ACKNOWLEDGEMENT

I would like to thank the following for their vital contributions:-
Beta reader, supporter and copyeditor - Linda Oliver
Proof-readers- Shirley de Vivo and Richard Walker
Cover designer – Cathy Walker (www.cathyscovers.wix.com)

A LIGHT IN THE DARK AGES SERIES

Follow the adventure in books two and three in the series:
Ambrosius: Last of the Romans - http://myBook.to/Ambrosius
Uther's Destiny - http://myBook.to/Uther

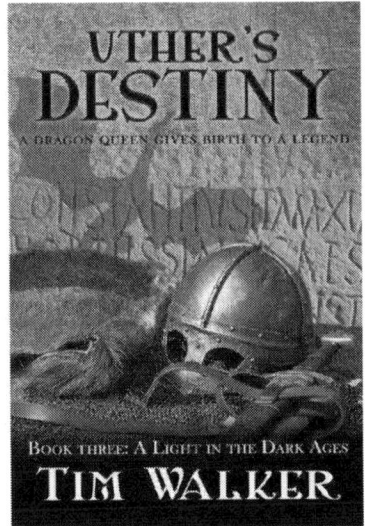

For news and to follow Tim Walker on social media:-
Author website: https://timwalkerwrites.co.uk
FaceBook: https://facebook.com/timwalkerwrites
Twitter: https://twitter.com/timwalker1666
Amazon Author Page: https://Author.to/TimWalkerWrites
Goodreads:
https://goodreads.com/author/show/678710.Tim_Walker

15658466R00116

Printed in Great Britain
by Amazon